# THE GEM

FOXGLOVES REGENCY ROMANCE BOOK 2

K.P. MARCH

Book Cover by Luisa Galstyan

First Edition: August 2025

Identifiers: 979-8-9922989-2-5 (paperback); 979-8-9922989-3-2 (ebook)

❀ Created with Vellum

*For the survivors, those still healing, and those who love them.*

*And for David.*

# WARNING

This story includes instances of parental abuse. Scenes containing emotional and physical abuse are not depicted, but they are recounted through several flashbacks.

The FMC is a survivor. She struggled in her young life, coming through to the other side a strong, fierce woman. The MMC is exceptionally kind. He is understanding, supportive, and the rock of this story.

This is a standalone book in an interconnected series. Guaranteed HEA. You will see Genevieve and Oliver again as side characters in future books.

# CHAPTER 1

## GENEVIEVE



"George, not so close to the lake," Genevieve called, watching her nephew's unstable toddler legs carry him closer and closer to the body of water. Hearing his aunt's voice, though, he turned in her direction, gave her a happy smile that made her heart swell, and began ambling back towards her.

"My goodness, he is a spirited one," Mrs. Potters, her old governess and now the children's nanny, commented her usual refrain as she held the sleeping Guinevere in her arms. They sat together under the strong, comforting branches of the oak tree near the Birmingham Estate grounds, the grass and flowers stretching out between them and the lake. They could see the Estate beyond it, standing proud and regal, the light from the clear day making it almost glitter like the surface of the water.

George tottered over to them, his burnished gold hair shining in the sun's light. He was the absolute image of his mother, Genevieve's sister-in-law, Amelia. Almost every day,

Genevieve could see him growing further into her features, and it amazed her how well they suited the little boy.

George's younger sister, Guinevere, was still too small and too new to start cataloguing most of her face, but if her dark hair and bright green eyes, the exact shape and color of Genevieve's brother, Gideon, were any indication, she would be taking after the Edwards side of her parentage.

"He is exceptionally spirited," Genevieve agreed, her regular reply to Mrs. Potters. "You are," she told George as he fell into her arms. "Aren't you, Georgie? Full of spirit and mischief and giggles." She tickled his belly as she spoke, and George disintegrated into a fit of giggles in her lap.

She could not believe how much her life had changed. That her family dynamic could be so full of happiness, laughter, and love.

Genevieve and Gideon rarely spoke of their childhoods or their parents, but they each carried their own sets of scars from them. Gideon's seemed to be mostly from their mother, who died when Genevieve was one, sending then seventeen-year-old Gideon running out of England. Genevieve did not blame him. Given half a chance, she would have done the same, and nothing and no one could have stopped her.

But that was not her story. No, Genevieve's story was shaped instead by their father, the late Duke of Birmingham, who raised her for the next nine years of her life until his death. Although, "raised her" was putting it generously. By then, ten-year-old Genevieve had long since learned how to keep herself small. Quiet. Pulled safely into herself and hidden so thoroughly that even she almost forgot who she was.

Almost.

When Gideon returned upon their father's death eight years ago, the siblings had been nervous and wary of one another, but with time, they came to trust and love each other deeply. Then, two years ago, Amelia brought her gentle sunshine into their still too dark home, showering Genevieve with her unwavering, unconditional love and acceptance.

It wasn't until Genevieve became an aunt, however, that she finally let go of her shell. She loved being an aunt. When she held George for the first time, someone fresh, pure, and a part of her, she had felt almost whole.

Almost.

# CHAPTER 2

## OLIVER

Oliver barely registered the home he'd been away from for the past seven years as he walked through it. Impatience coursed through him as he followed Smith, their country butler, towards the drawing room. For seven years, he had not been in a rush. Even when he was in London with his brother this past week, he hadn't felt this urgency. Now that he was so close, however, it felt like seven years' worth of it was pounding through him, making him want to run in his haste.

Which was why upon entering the drawing room and seeing his mother jump up from the dark pastel couch, her eyes bright as they landed on him, Oliver moved to her swiftly. She had aged, but he didn't pause to catalogue the changes in the beautiful Prudence Sinclair yet.

Oliver embraced her and kissed her soft cheek before murmuring, "Please excuse me, Mother. I will be right back."

Then, he turned around and strode from the room just as quickly as he'd entered it. He followed his feet as they led him down the familiar path to Sinclair Manor's back door. Oliver still did not notice a thing about his surroundings. His mind singularly focused on his destination.

He could still remember it. That day, thirteen years ago. When he made this same walk out of this same door, not anticipating what awaited him. And now, his feet led him with an eagerness he could not contain right back to that spot. To what waited for him there.

*OLIVER WAS RUNNING, his energy boundless and too much for his twelve-year-old body to contain. He cut across the grass, past the oak tree, the flowers a blur at the edges of his vision, and headed straight for the lake. He was running so fast, he had to skid to a halt to keep from sliding right into the body of water that separated his family's grounds from the Birmingham Estate grounds.*

*He immediately started circling around the lake, eyes fixed to the ground as he searched between the blades of grass and flowers for rocks that would suit his purpose. He gathered them in his cupped hand, propping the pile against his stomach as it grew. Once both hands were almost overflowing, he went back to the edge of the lake and settled in for his task.*

*One by one, he angled his body, whipping the rocks sideways at the water, only for each one to fall directly into it with a loud* plunk. *Not a single rock skipped. With every failed throw, he grew more and more annoyed, not understanding why it wasn't working. The sun warmed the back of his neck, the wind ruffling gently through his hair, as he determinedly tossed rock after rock at the water with very little success.*

*How had Charles done it? Oliver would never ask him, but he wondered at it with increasing aggravation. If he did ask his older brother for help, he would only tease him relentlessly for not knowing.*

*Frustrated, Oliver chucked the last rock at the water, effectively splashing himself. He lowered down into a crouch with a huff, the front of his clothes now wet, and wrapped his arms around his knees.*

*There was nothing else for it. He needed more rocks.*

*Standing back up, Oliver turned around, and that's when he saw her. A tiny little thing was huddled underneath the branches of the large oak tree he had run past. He hadn't noticed her at all.*

*How long had she been there? Had she seen him fail so spectacularly at trying to skip rocks? The way her face tilted in his direction, she must have been watching him and seen everything. Oliver felt his cheeks warm as he stepped over the grass and made his way towards her.*

*The little girl didn't move as he approached. Wrapped around herself, Oliver got the sense that she was trying to shrink down as small as she possibly could. Her hair was dark and shiny, like black silk, and made the part of her face not tucked behind her knees look extra pale. Not in a bad way, he noted. She didn't look sick, just very fair.*

*It was her eyes, though. Her eyes were dark. So dark, they looked black, and they were fixed on him as if they had hooked right into him. How could a little child look like that? Did she even blink? Something in her gaze looked...sad. Heavy. Too heavy for such a small person. It unnerved him, but still he stepped forward without hesitation.*

*"Good morning," Oliver said, coming to stand beside where she nestled into the roots of the oak tree.*

*Her eyes stayed firmly fixed on him, but she didn't lift her head or answer or give any indication that she heard him speak.*

*"I am Oliver Sinclair," he continued undeterred when she did not return his greeting. "What's your name?"*

*Still, the little wraith said nothing. Just watched. She observed him so intently, he was sure no one had ever examined him that closely before. He felt a prickling of discomfort but trudged through it.*

*"Are you sad?" he asked bluntly, trying to understand the look in her eyes and the way she watched him.*

*The odd girl only stared at him in reply.*

*Oliver assessed her for another moment, then, coming to a decision, he turned and walked through the grass once more. Only this time, he collected the flowers that sprouted all around the lake instead* of gathering rocks. Once he felt he had collected a satisfactory amount, he made his way back to the girl and held them out to her.

Her eyes went to his offering before lifting back to his face. Oliver remained quiet, not saying anything further as he kept the flowers extended.

Very slowly, she put out a little hand and took them.

Oliver felt an odd rush of relief.

"They're foxgloves," he told her. "My mother loves them."

Finally, the little girl lifted her head to timidly hold her face into the bouquet he'd collected for her. That's when Oliver noticed the angry red mark on her left cheek. As if she'd been struck. And struck hard.

He wanted to ask her if she was okay but knew intuitively that if he did, she'd shrink back into that little ball in the roots of the tree, all the progress made from the flowers forgotten.

"Foxgloves," she repeated in a sweet, little girl's lilt. Oliver couldn't help but find her absolutely adorable. "They're pretty."

"Like you," he replied both with kindness and honesty.

Her eyes snapped back to him, and he was struck again by the thought that those eyes did not seem right for a child. Probably because her world left her with marks on her face and heaven only knew what else.

"Won't you tell me your name?" he tried again.

The little girl paused, considering the flowers once more, and Oliver was sure she would let the question go unanswered yet again when she finally murmured, "Genevieve."

"Genevieve," he tried it out. "Genevieve what?"

"Edwards," she answered quicker this time.

Genevieve Edwards. She was the Duke of Birmingham's daughter.

Oliver experienced his first moment of pause as he wondered if he should be speaking to her. Was he allowed to speak to a duke's daughter? His father didn't hold a title, and Oliver was only the second son. He probably wasn't allowed to speak to her at all.

"How old are you?" he asked her more cautiously.

"Five," she replied in that sweet voice.

He felt an odd tenderness for this tiny, hurt child sitting all alone at the bottom of a tree with no one to comfort her after whatever had happened. He decided it was worth the risk of getting in trouble as he spoke again.

"I'm trying to skip rocks. Want to help me?" Oliver offered her his friendship, something he could sense this girl needed greatly and perhaps didn't even realize. She was so terribly small after all.

"I don't know how," she informed him innocently.

"Me either." Oliver shrugged before assuring her, "We can learn together."

Without another word, she stood up, clutching her foxgloves in one of her little hands, and looked at him expectantly.

He grinned at her. "First, we need to find more rocks."

# CHAPTER 3

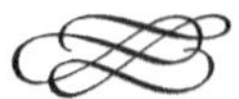

GENEVIEVE

"I think it's time for Miss Guinevere to go in," Mrs. Potters said to Genevieve as she lay forward on her elbows, diligently collecting the blades of grass George plucked and handed to her in his own game.

Genevieve looked over her shoulder and saw her niece had started to fuss quietly, squirming in the blanket she was wrapped in.

She turned back to her nephew. "Let's go play inside, Georgie," she said. His little face started to contort with refusal, so Genevieve added quickly, "Your sister is tired and needs to rest in her bed. We want to take care of her, don't we?"

His light chocolate eyes looked over at the bundle his nanny held. Genevieve could tell he was internally debating whether to put his little foot down to stay outside or give his sister what she wanted. George was still in the process of deciding if he liked his new sister or not. Today, it seemed he did as he abandoned the grass in his hand and stood up.

Genevieve smiled, carefully placing the blades of grass she cupped safely amongst the roots of the tree. They'd be long gone by the time they came out next and George will have forgotten, but for now, he was watching her, and she would not carelessly toss away the gifts he'd collected for her. She stood up, as did Mrs. Potters, both grateful for his easy acquiescence, however short lived it may be.

"Shall I take her, Mrs. Potters?" Genevieve asked, offering the nanny a chance to rest her arms, while also hopefully helping Guinevere settle. Mrs. Potters handed the baby over with an appreciative smile. Genevieve began lightly rocking her niece as they walked back towards the Birmingham Estate, George holding Mrs. Potters's hand.

"There, there, little one," Genevieve cooed. "Everything's alright." Guinevere cracked her emerald eyes and focused in on her aunt. "That's right," Genevieve smiled at her, stroking her soft baby cheek with her index finger. "See? Nothing to worry about."

The group had made its way to the other side of the lake and were just about to enter the Birmingham Estate grounds when a voice stopped her dead in her tracks. Her breath caught in her chest, and she forgot how to push air in and out of her lungs altogether.

"Genevieve."

The single word was said quietly, but he could have screamed it in Genevieve's face for all its impact. She knew who called to her. There was only one boy who ever met her here. Even if the voice sounded different now from how she remembered it. Deeper. Rougher. But still comforting. Still sweet.

Mrs. Potters, who had been walking next to her with George, stopped and gave her a quizzical look before her gaze shifted to over Genevieve's shoulder. To the person who'd come from the direction of Sinclair Manor on the other side of the oak tree.

Genevieve heard his approach, her heart racing. Her emotions rioting. Her anger burning.

How *dare* he come back? How dare he come here? How dare he call her name?

She looked up instinctively when she saw movement enter her field of vision, and she was shocked by how much he'd changed. Gone was the beautiful young boy she had always thought pretty and had loved dearly with her tender, broken child's heart. In his place stood a man. Rugged and honed. His features strong and masculine. His rich brown hair was short and wavy. Windswept, like he'd walked straight off a ship at sea only moments ago, the shiny locks moving gently in the soft breeze of the day. His face was covered by a short beard, and it suited him so much that Genevieve felt something stir within her at the sight. She wanted to feel the short bristles against her fingertips. And that just made her all the angrier.

The sun shined on his already tanned skin. As if he had spent the past few years kissed by it daily on his adventures. Few years, she thought bitterly. It was seven. Seven years, four months, and three and a half weeks.

Those deep blue eyes were also older, the very first hints of lines crinkling them at the edges. They felt worldlier now as he looked at her. The ocean of his gaze holding greater depths than before he left. But they were also still him. Still generous and open and accepting.

Oliver had become a man in their years apart. A well-built man, if the muscles obvious through his traveling clothes were anything to go off. He would make any woman's mouth water at the sight of him.

Genevieve, however, narrowed her eyes.

She hated the changes as she admired them, too. She hated that he *was* handsome. That he had grown. That he was different from the boy she knew, and yet still somehow exactly the same. She didn't know which bothered her more. Perhaps it was everything. Everything about him as he stood there, breathtaking and beautiful and older and him.

She didn't say a word, eyeing him as he stopped before her. His eyes went to Guinevere, now snug and quiet in her aunt's arms, and then to George, hiding behind Mrs. Potters's skirts.

"You have children." It was a statement, and Genevieve was overcome with the urge to slap his presumptuous, arrogantly assuming, only just returned, stupidly handsome face. He had the nerve to sound almost angry. Like he had any right to. The bastard.

"These are the Duke and Duchess of Birmingham's children, Sir," Mrs. Potters clarified for him.

Oliver turned to the woman and seemed to remember his manners. One side of his lips pulled up in a deliciously charming smirk. Genevieve was sure that smirk would have more than one woman sighing at the sight. "Apologies, madam," he said in a voice smooth as silk while giving her a small bow. "I have not introduced myself. I am Oliver Sinclair. I grew up just on the other side of the lake, at Sinclair Manor."

Oliver had always been a confident boy. Unassumingly kind. It seemed he'd grown further into that confidence as a man, wearing it easily, like a second skin. Now, he was *charming*. She could still feel that quality in his presence, the uniquely Oliver one, that made you want to trust him, to believe him, just by being near him.

Genevieve knew better now.

"Ah, Mr. Sinclair, yes," Genevieve could hear the smile in Mrs. Potters's voice, but she didn't turn to look. Her eyes still watched the man that thought it prudent to seek her out after being away for over seven years. The nanny continued, "It is wonderful to make your acquaintance. I am Mrs. Potters, the children's nanny and Lady Genevieve's former governess. She and I have often visited your mother these past years."

"You have?" Oliver's deep blue eyes shot back to Genevieve, who had yet to look away from him. Not that she had any intention to. Let him squirm as she peeled back his layers with her scrutiny. Let him be unnerved and uncomfortable under her unwavering gaze.

"Yes," Mrs. Potters answered again when Genevieve remained silent. "We have met your brother, of course, but I am sorry to say I have not heard of you. I imagine you have been abroad? Perhaps it pained your mother to speak of you in your absence."

Oliver listened but assessed Genevieve. She didn't break the contact. Like hell would she be the one to look away first. Like. Hell.

"Yes, perhaps," he agreed, and the way he observed Genevieve made her think he knew exactly for *whom* it would have been too painful to speak of him. She felt her blood pound harder in her chest as her anger continued to escalate.

He broke their staring contest first, like she knew he would. "These are His Grace's children, you say?" he asked, turning back to Mrs. Potters, clearly understanding if he wanted answers, he'd have better luck with her. Not the silent, watchful woman currently glaring daggers at him.

"Yes," she smiled. "This is Master George," Genevieve saw Mrs. Potters's hand move to George's back, introducing the boy that was watching everything keenly from behind the safety of his nanny's dress. Her other hand then waved towards the bundle in Genevieve's arms. "And that is Miss Guinevere."

"Guinevere," he tried out the name. "A Welsh name. Oddly reminiscent of Genevieve, no?" The bastard gave her an endearingly uncertain smile, and Genevieve felt a scream of fury build up in her chest in response.

"Why, yes," Mrs. Potters replied, pleased. "Most people think it unusual she was given a Welsh name, but she was, indeed, named for Lady Genevieve."

Damn him.

Oliver's smile wavered in the face of Genevieve's silent wrath. Abandoning that, he decided to try his charms elsewhere. He crouched down in the grass, one arm bent over his knee, the fingertips of the other braced against the ground. He faced George and smiled stunningly.

"Good day, little Lord," Oliver spoke to George. "Won't you come out and meet me?"

That did it. Genevieve felt herself snap. The way he knelt down. The way he smiled. The easy, open way he spoke to George. The question, so very close to how he'd first spoken to her the day she met him.

*Damn him.*

# CHAPTER 4

## OLIVER

"We're leaving," Genevieve finally spoke for the first time. Her voice was high and sweet, even in its currently scathing tone. She was around him in a second, barely allowing him time to stand up before she passed him. He could smell jasmine in the air as she stirred it, and his senses heightened at the beautiful fragrance.

Even her voice and scent, he found lovely.

"Gen," Oliver began, standing quickly and facing the direction of her retreating back. The familiarity of the nickname had her rounding on him, her fury a living thing he could feel between them. He had never seen her so mad, not like this. Full of pure rage.

"*Don't,*" she hissed. "Don't you dare, Oliver Sinclair."

"Lady Genevieve," the pleasant Mrs. Potters, who had thus far been the only one talking to him, now spoke more cautiously, finally sensing the nature of this reunion. "Perhaps I should take the children inside."

Genevieve only responded by wordlessly handing over the baby in her arms without lifting the glare she aimed at Oliver.

She was so much the same, and yet so entirely different.

Oliver had been shocked to come upon her. He hadn't been expecting his luck. The chances of her being here the moment he returned seemed so slim. But of course, he hoped for it. It's why he'd come here without delay, having just arrived home.

When he rounded the oak tree and first saw her, he thought she was a dream. Walking around the lake where they'd first met and spent so many of their days. The sun shining off her dark, silken hair that hung loose down her back. Her body long and steps graceful in her pale blue dress. She was surrounded by children. A little boy at her feet, a baby in her arms that she was stroking and rocking as she walked, a soft smile on her lips. Oliver was surprised by what the whole image ignited in him. An immediate and undeniable feeling of *want*.

She'd always been the sweet, hurting little girl that only he could make smile. Now....

Now, that little girl was a woman. Tall. Regal. Her body and face slim with bow lips and sharp features, from the cut of her nose to the angles of her cheekbones and jaw line. Everything about her could only be described as striking. Like a fine blade. The kind that made you stop and admire the craftsmanship that created something so beautiful, so lethal. Even in the way she scowled at him, Genevieve was breathtaking. In fact, he realized somewhat shocked, he'd never seen a more beautiful, more exquisite woman.

Once he'd recovered from admiring her changes, he was surprised still further to think she was now married and a mother. It had to be too fast. She was only eighteen. Thanks to the helpful Mrs. Potters, however, he was relieved to learn of his mistake.

As Mrs. Potters had continued to speak to him, he began noticing the similarities between the beauty before him and the child from his memories. It was in those eyes. Those too heavy, dark, black eyes that still felt like they'd seen too much. Knew too much. Saw too much. And she was looking at him like she had the first day he'd met her. Silent and observant. Distrustful.

No, there was more to it now, he realized, feeling the weight of her glare as they finally stood alone. The nanny and children had left, making their way back to the Birmingham Estate.

No, now there was distrust in those eyes and *hate*.

He could guess why. The same reason she'd apparently kept up visits to his mother, which the latter had conveniently neglected to mention in her many letters to him these past years. Oliver felt a slight touch of guilt that he'd never written to Genevieve to hear this directly from her. But how could he have? With the new Duke of Birmingham having just returned to the country before Oliver left, it would have been improper for him to see his sister corresponding with the neighbor's younger boy.

What's more, Oliver knew before he left that Genevieve had developed an extra fondness for him. But she'd been a child. He assumed her crush would fade while they were apart and she grew up, the way most childish things do. Looking at her now, Oliver acknowledged that he probably should have known better. This was Genevieve after all. She'd never been allowed to be a normal child. She wouldn't let go of things as a normal child might.

"You seem upset," he finally broke the silence that had settled between them as they continued to face off. He could see the nanny and her charges almost at the Estate by now.

As soon as he spoke the words, however, he knew he'd said the wrong thing. He did not think it possible for her expression to darken further.

This woman was *spitting* mad.

"Do I?" she seethed. "I'm surprised you are even able to notice, given how self-absorbed you are."

Oliver blinked in surprise before feeling his own anger start to rise up. "Excuse me?" he said, his voice coming out somewhat sharper after her insult.

"You heard me," she spat. "I don't know what you're doing back or why you thought it wise to seek me out, and frankly, I don't care. I have no desire to speak with you, Mr. Sinclair, and I want nothing but for you to leave me the hell alone."

Not giving him the opportunity to reply, she spun on her heel and left, stoking his anger further. She wasn't even going to let him speak?

He watched her go, his jaw clenching. Oliver hated how he admired the grace with which she stormed away.

She hadn't even talked to him. Hadn't asked where he'd been, what he'd seen, given him the chance to ask after her. Her brother, sister-in-law, their children. What her family was like now. How she felt about it. She hadn't welcomed him back at all. Just insulted him, in a most unladylike but wholly Genevieve manner, and stalked off.

This was not what he had been expecting. The quiet little girl of his memories was now an elegant, rude, and self-righteous woman. She truly was stunning. Both in her beauty and in her pride. And she'd been entirely unimpressed by his looks, charms, and teasing.

Oliver turned around and made his way to the edge of the lake, picking up an appropriate rock from among the blades of grass as he went.

To hell with her. Beautiful or not. History or not. Who was she to do nothing but glower at him with hatred after seven years apart before insulting him and stalking off, not even allowing him a chance to defend himself?

Angling to the side, he threw the rock, watching it skip across the still surface.

He sighed, leaning his head back and closing his eyes as he faced the sky. He felt an errant thought run through his mind.

Foxgloves probably wouldn't work this time.

# CHAPTER 5

## GENEVIEVE

Genevieve felt her hard footsteps against the grass as she trekked back home. Without breaking stride, she walked inside and straight through the hall. Her feet pounded up the stairs until she finally reached and shut herself inside the safety of her bedroom. She was so angry, the edges of her vision were blurring. She didn't even know if she passed anyone on the way to her room, but if she had, they wisely did not stop her.

Inside her bedroom, she continued pacing, back and forth across the floor, her hands planted on her hips as she tried fruit-lessly to catch her breath. To contain the emotions roiling within her. To stop *feeling*.

But Oliver had always made her feel. As much as she'd protected herself by locking up her emotions carefully out of sight, he would always bring them out. And she had never known what to do with them, the things she felt, the things he encouraged from her. Just like now. She did not know how to manage the fury coursing through her, but she knew she needed to keep her focus on it. Stay in that space until she could safely shove the feelings back into their box. The anger, and the pain it concealed.

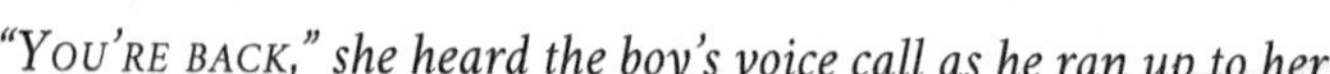

"YOU'RE BACK," *she heard the boy's voice call as he ran up to her.*

*Of course, she'd come back. He had to know she would by now. She'd come back multiple times, and each day, he commented on it with the same happy surprise, as if he didn't think she'd actually return. Sure, she still didn't speak to him very much, and he still scared her a little bit, but so far, he'd been nice to her. Of course, she was going to keep coming back. At least until he wasn't nice anymore.*

*"You're here," he panted, stopping before her where she waited for him. She sat on the ground in her usual spot under the big, safe oak tree. No one knew of her spot. No one except this strange, nice boy, who seemed to like her.*

*"I am," she answered him, standing up and facing him.*

*He positively beamed at her. He seemed truly delighted that he no longer had to coax her into replying. As if her interacting with him brought him genuine joy.*

*Genevieve felt an odd sort of feeling. Her face grew a little warm. She didn't know what this was, but she didn't say anything. She just watched the boy that might be her friend and tried not to feel whatever it was she was feeling.*

*"What should we do today?" he asked her, looking around him for inspiration, his arms swinging very slightly as he did so.*

*She waited for him to arrive at an activity, like he always did. Since that first day, they'd skipped rocks (she still couldn't); played races from the oak tree to the lake (Oliver always won); tried to climb the oak tree (neither could reach even the lowest branches); looked for treasures amongst the grass and flowers (there was none); followed the path of insects among the oak roots while imagining the stories of their insect lives (Oliver's were much more imaginative). It seemed Oliver had an endless number of things for them to do, which was all well* since Genevieve could only ever think to sit quietly in the shelter of her tree.

"I know," he finally exclaimed, turning his dark blue eyes on her, bright with inspiration. His grin still split his face in two. "How about we swim?"

"I don't know how to swim," Genevieve told him. She never felt shy about admitting how little she knew. It did not even occur to her to feel embarrassed about it. She was usually her own company after all, at least until recently when she met this boy. But there had never been anyone around to judge her for not knowing things.

"I'll teach you," he replied, already turning and walking through the grass and flowers, covering the distance to the lake. She followed him without hesitation.

He sat down at the water's edge and began peeling off his shoes. Genevieve did the same, sitting down beside him. He then stood and took off his clothes until he wore only his undergarments.

"We have to take off our clothes?" she asked, standing up and already wiggling out of her dress.

"Of course, silly Genny," he shook his head. "We can't swim in our clothes. They'd get all wet."

A moment later, they were both in their undergarments and he was holding her hand, leading her slowly into the water. Genevieve felt her heart start to stutter in a way she knew well as she stepped further and further into the water.

Fear.

But she didn't tell him. She just kept her grip tight on his hand with her little fingers and took step after step, the water inching closer to her face with each one. She was so much smaller than Oliver that by the time it was up to her chin, it was only halfway up his torso.

"Now, be sure to wave your arms and legs back and forth once you no longer feel the ground anymore. And don't be afraid. I'm right here. I won't let anything happen to you."

She stared at his face, his pretty blue eyes, deciding if he was telling the truth or not. He looked back unfazed, completely reassuring. He *didn't rush her, but simply kept eye contact and let her see and decide whatever she needed.*

*She decided she believed him.*

*Following his direction and keeping her eyes fixed on him, she stepped forward, losing the ground if she wanted to keep her head above the water.*

*Genevieve followed each of Oliver's directions, and before she knew it, she was farther into the lake and swimming. Between Oliver's guidance and some sort of instinct, she took to swimming like she imagined a fish would. Maybe she could be a fish. Just live in this lake by her safe oak, and Oliver could come visit her.*

*"Gen, you're doing it," Oliver praised her so generously as he instructed her, she felt something sparkle inside her at his words. "You're doing so well. Like you were meant to swim."*

*She did something then that she couldn't remember ever doing before, but she did it without thought. Without realizing it. On instinct, like paddling her limbs.*

*Bobbing up and down in the water, Genevieve looked over at the bizarre boy that was kind.*

*And she smiled.*

# CHAPTER 6

## OLIVER

"Mother." Oliver drew his mother's attention from where she sat embroidering on the couch as he once again entered the drawing room of Sinclair Manor, his excitement significantly dampened over the last half hour.

This time, he took her and the room in with more care. She looked older, seven years having grayed much of her blonde hair. Her fine features were accented with more wrinkles, but those baby blue eyes were as mischievous as ever before. The room, on the other hand, was exactly how he remembered it. The light brown wallpaper that brightened in the light from the large windows, but also enveloped occupants in warmth during the evenings. The intricate cream and gold edged trim around the room; the dark, heavy, and currently open curtains; the assortment of dark pastel couches; the flower arrangements and fine, decorative trinkets on the various tabletops around the room. The fireplace his mother sat facing was unlit, and the few, tasteful paintings along the walls were unchanged. He immediately crossed the room to the corner side table and poured himself a drink.

It had been a long journey, and his reunion with Genevieve

was less than pleasant. The irritation and dejection still coursed through him. He took a sip, stepping back towards the seating area and his mother.

"You're back," his mother smiled at him like she'd never been happier. Her eyes were bright and full of love, and his heart thawed some after the chill it caught from his interaction with Genevieve. His mother, at least, had missed him and was happy to see him returned. She continued speaking. "Did you find what you went searching for when you ran out of here with barely a kiss to your mother's cheek after seven long years?" she teased him.

"I see my time away has done nothing to dull your theatrics," he rolled his eyes, standing beside the couch, drink in hand.

"On the contrary, dear, I find old age to have freed me more than anything," she told him cheerfully. Laying her embroidery on the table beside her, she patted the seat cushion on her other side for Oliver to sit.

He obliged, leaning fully back and stretching out his long legs as he relaxed, his drink resting against his thigh. His eyes were trained forward, and his mother let him take a moment of pause like she used to do when she sensed he needed to gather his thoughts.

"Why did you not tell me she would visit you?" Oliver finally asked, eyes still gazing forward. He didn't bother to specify who he meant. They both knew.

"It seemed she did not want me to," she answered honestly.

"What do you mean?" Oliver turned his head and looked at his mother.

"Well, it was clear when she first started to visit me with her governess, she was here because she missed you. But even at the age of…what, eleven? Twelve?"

"Ten," he corrected automatically.

"Right, ten," his mother's eyes sparked knowingly. "Well,

even then, she never once asked after you. And truth be told, I don't think I've ever seen a child so lonely before."

Oliver's heart clenched. He lifted his glass and took a drink, eyes breaking away again.

"Well, I just didn't want to be yet another person in her life that broke her trust. Even if she would never know about it, I just couldn't do that to her."

"Are you implying that *I* broke her trust?" he challenged.

"Of course, you did," she replied matter-of-factly, and Oliver felt himself bristle. "Don't mistake me, Oliver dear, I know it was not your intent. Nor was it your responsibility to stay here for the late Duke of Birmingham's daughter. It had always been important to you, ever since you were very little, to make your own way after living in Charles's shadow and perhaps also Genevieve's. You deserved to go out and find your own place in the world. But the other side of that coin is what your departure did to that fragile girl. I think she quite loved you, of course, but that was always secondary. More than that, I think you were all she had up until that point. That's why she came here after you left. I don't think she had anywhere else to go."

Oliver absorbed his mother's words alongside the liquor that burned down his chest with another sip. Of course, she was right about his drive to leave. He'd never made a secret of it. He did not run away – he simply left to become something more than the second son of a wealthy businessman. Someone that could talk to a peer of the realm and their family without a second thought. He always intended to return once his mission had been accomplished.

But he wasn't sure what to make of how his departure impacted Genevieve. He'd always thought of her fondly during his years away and knew she had an unfairly, terribly tough young life, but he never actually considered that his absence would alter her in any real way. Even as they grew as children and friends, he knew how far beneath her he was. For him to be able to affect her so deeply had been unfathomable to him. The ignorance of youth, he supposed. Perhaps she might not have been too off the mark by calling him self-absorbed. It was a bitter thought to admit to himself.

"That doesn't seem to be the case anymore, though," Oliver probed after a moment.

"Oh, no, not at all," his mother picked her embroidery back up, resuming her stitching as she sensed the difficult part of the conversation had passed. "The new Duke of Birmingham… although, he's not new anymore, is he? It's been eight or so years now since he took up the title. Anyhow, he loves her dearly. It's quite sweet to see the two of them together and how much they've both grown. He's had quite a bit of difficulty, too, much like Genevieve, because of their late parents, may they rest in hell. But the two of them seem to have found a way to heal together. The lovely Duchess of Birmingham has definitely helped them both in that regard. And of course, there are also the little ones now. Young George absolutely adores Genevieve, and I'm sure the new baby will, as well. She dotes on them, you see. No, her family home is quite different now, thank heavens."

"I'm glad to hear it," Oliver commented absentmindedly. He was, truly, immensely glad to hear it. Yet, he felt something weighing on him. He couldn't identify or understand it.

Well, he thought, emptying the contents of his glass, whatever the past, the Genevieve of today had been quite transparent in her loathing of him. He was none too impressed with her and her offensive manner either, even if he felt the little boy in him itching to make her like him again. It didn't matter what the little boy wanted. He wasn't that boy anymore, nor was she that little girl. Clearly.

"You best get ready, dear," his mother interrupted his reverie.

"For what?" he turned to her.

"For dinner, of course," she said without looking up from the design she was stitching into existence with her needle.

"I have plenty of time," he replied.

"Oh, no, you don't. I have invited the Birminghams. You need to clean up properly before you meet Their Graces."

What? No. How could he see Genevieve again after the way she'd declared she wanted nothing to do with him? Besides, with how passionately she hated him, the duke and duchess would hardly be inclined to take a shine to him.

"Mother," he started, sitting up to argue with her properly.

"It's fixed now, dear, so you'd better get ready instead of wasting your breath resisting it."

Damn it.

# CHAPTER 7

## GENEVIEVE

This was the last thing she wanted to be doing tonight, Genevieve thought to herself as she stepped out of the carriage after Amelia. She stared up at Sinclair Manor with its glowing lights and beautiful details carved carefully into the stone and archways. This place had filled her emptiness with warmth and comfort these past years, and now she felt the dread already gathered in the pit of her stomach intensifying. Ironically, that dread now was at the prospect of facing the very man whose absence had caused the emptiness to begin with.

She'd had no choice but to come tonight. When the invitation arrived, which of course it did, Gideon and Amelia accepted, which of course they did. She couldn't very well tell them she refused to see the guest of honor. Someone who, as far as either of them knew, was a stranger to her, and she was not interested in correcting that assumption.

"Everything alright, Genevieve?" Amelia asked, leaning forward to look at her around Gideon as he escorted them up the Manor steps.

Gideon turned to look at Genevieve.

*Damn.*

"Is something wrong?" her brother asked.

Trust Amelia to notice Genevieve's withdrawn behavior. She was falling back on old habits. She knew that. Retreating into herself. She had to get it together. She'd be damned if she let that bastard Oliver ruin her evening.

"Everything's fine," she forced her lips to pull up. "What could possibly be wrong?" Her voice sounded false even to her own ears.

They clearly weren't convinced either with the way Amelia's brow pinched slightly and Gideon's eyes narrowed. They didn't push it, though, as they entered Sinclair Manor and were greeted by Smith, who smiled warmly at Genevieve and Amelia, both of whom were frequent visitors of the Manor.

Genevieve focused on keeping her heart rate steady and appearing cool and unfazed as they were led to the drawing room. The anticipation of what awaited her in the room made the short, familiar walk seem endless, taking at least thrice as long.

The room was warm, lit by the soft glow of candles and the fire burning in the fireplace. She'd been in this very room, sat on these very couches, drank tea with Prudence Sinclair hundreds, thousands of times, and yet….

Yet, this room had never felt so new to her, so irritatingly inviting, as it did tonight. With the tall, impeccably dressed man leaning against the mantle.

Genevieve's eyes had searched and found him almost immediately upon walking through the drawing room door. He'd changed from his traveling clothes into rich evening attire that fit his strong body snugly. His hair and beard were groomed, but the wild edge they gave him couldn't be tamed. Instead, it added to his allure as a rough, worldly, sophisticated man. Her mouth watered at his physique and severe, forbidden beauty. She felt her nervous heartbeat transform and race for an entirely different reason.

Her gaze finally tracked to his, and Genevieve found his dark blue eyes already on her, watching how she appraised his whole body, top to bottom. The desire she felt stirring within her quickly shifted back to disdain.

Bastard, she thought. Watching her as she drank him in with her eyes.

"Your Graces," Prudence's voice finally pulled Genevieve's awareness to the rest of the room. She had lingered in the entrance of the drawing room, eyes fixed to the insufferable man who had finally deemed it time to return home and talk to her, and she hadn't observed any of her other surroundings. Smith had already left after announcing them to make final dinner preparations, and Prudence stood in front of the not quite pale blue couch.

Genevieve quickly followed her brother and sister-in-law into the room and greeted their hostess, hoping no one else noticed her delay and the reason for it.

"And this is my younger son, Oliver, who I don't believe you have met before. He's only just returned from several years abroad."

Oliver stepped forward, bowing to Amelia and giving her hand a kiss, before turning to bow to Gideon with a murmured "Your Grace" to each.

Gideon replied by taking the younger man's hand and shaking it in an uncharacteristic display of friendliness. He studied Oliver politely as he answered Prudence, "No, we haven't yet had the pleasure. But I have met your brother a few times. He's currently in London, is he not?"

"Yes, Your Grace," Oliver answered in his deep, sensual voice. Genevieve hated how her core clenched at the sound. "I spent a few days with him before returning home earlier today."

Genevieve took a seat next to Prudence as Amelia occupied the brown, intricately embroidered armchair on their hostess's other side. The two men continued to discuss London and Oliver's brother, Charles, who tended to spend most of his days there recently. His wedding to Anna Lucas, the daughter and only child of the Earl and Countess of Dunhill, was fast approaching, planned for just before Christmastime this year. It was an arrangement made between their two families many, many years ago. Charles, it seemed, was thus eager to soak up as many months of freedom left to him before he was obliged to return home and run Sinclair Manor with his wife.

"How is your embroidery, Prudence?" Amelia asked.

"Oh, lovely, dear." Both Amelia and Prudence shared a mutual love of the art, and while Genevieve knew how to stitch a few very simple designs decently well, she found she lacked the visual creativity to make a design from nothing. She also didn't enjoy the activity, itself. It was too quiet. Too calm. Where one had nothing to do but *think*.

Genevieve instead preferred the piano. The music, beauty, and power of it. The way it could move between softness, pain, melancholy, joy, thrill, anger, rage, volatility. Through the keys and the notes, she could channel and expel her feelings in a way that was both manageable and beautiful. She could make sense of the world sitting at a piano bench, turning confusing, overwhelming emotions into something with meaning and splendor.

Prudence continued, "I shall show you my current project after dinner."

"I would be delighted if you would," Amelia smiled, a glimmer of eagerness in her soft brown eyes.

"And how are you, Genevieve dear?" Prudence turned to her.

People needed to stop asking such questions.

"I am well," Genevieve supplied succinctly.

"It must be nice to have your friend back home at long last," her hostess pushed, and Genevieve felt the breath catch in her chest and the weight of Amelia's gaze fall upon her.

"Not a friend," Genevieve clarified, looking only at

Prudence. From the corner of her eye, she noticed Oliver's head snap in her direction at her words, and her body warmed under his gaze. "Just a very old acquaintance I knew in passing during my youth."

Amelia tilted her head at Genevieve before turning back to Prudence with understanding. Her sister-in-law noticed far too much. Much more than Genevieve was ready to show or even examine herself.

"But it must be wonderful for you to have your son home after so long," Amelia shifted the focus easily. "I cannot imagine what I will do if my Georgie decides to go overseas for years."

"He won't," Gideon assured her from where he stood speaking with Oliver by the fireplace, as if he'd been part of the ladies' conversation all along. As always, he was perfectly attuned to his wife and she to him, even as they held completely separate conversations. Genevieve had never seen any two people as in sync or connected as deeply as her brother and his wife were to each other. And their bond only seemed to grow stronger the longer they were married.

"*You* did," Genevieve reminded him.

"Nor is it for you to decide," Amelia added before turning back to Prudence. "I'm sure you did not choose for your son to go off to sea."

"Certainly not," Prudence scoffed with feigned indignation. "I'd have kept him locked up safe at home if I could. But alas, mothers must let their children grow and make their own choices. Even if it kills them." She hammed up her last sentence, and Genevieve hid her chuckle at Prudence's theatrics behind a hand.

Again, she felt the heat of Oliver's gaze on her, and this time, she met it. If she did not know any better, she'd say his deep blue eyes were watching her with something akin to wonder.

Oliver blinked and turned to his mother. "Drama does not become you, Mother."

"Ha! I beg your pardon," she lifted her chin and somehow managed to look down her nose at her standing son from where she sat. "It most certainly does become me. I am quite the gifted actress."

Amelia and Genevieve laughed outright while Gideon chuckled at their colorful hostess.

"Clearly," Oliver muttered, but his eyes were once again watching Genevieve.

She chose to ignore him. She would be cold. Aloof. Indifferent to his wonder and whatever else.

Even if it killed her.

# CHAPTER 8

OLIVER

*D*amn it, but she was beautiful. She'd arrived with the Duke and Duchess of Birmingham, and since then, Oliver had been in a constant fight with his eyes to keep them from staring at her.

Her dress was a forest green, and it looked magnificent against her dark hair and eyes and pale skin. She was absolutely lovely. Ever the picturesque young lady, sister to a peer of the realm. And yet looking at her in her green dress, he kept thinking of how perfect she would look sitting in her spot under their oak tree, waiting for him. Grown and breathtaking and wholly her. *His gem.*

Oliver shook the thought away and finally acknowledged what he'd been denying since seeing her earlier that day. He was attracted to Genevieve. Painfully so. On the heels of that, he made sure to remind himself of the impossibility of anything coming of it. Even if she didn't detest him, he could never be with her. He was educated and independently rich, yes, having used his years of travel well and with purpose, but he was *still* only the second son of a wealthy, title-less estate. He always would be. Whereas *she* would always be a *lady*. Even if he wanted her, not that he did, he could never have her. It was one thing to befriend her in spite of their different stations, but quite another to pursue her. She was, as she'd always been, too far above his reach.

He focused on her brother, who was strikingly similar to her in appearance, and concentrated his energy on keeping his glances to her infrequent and brief. Although, it seemed she was the only place his eyes wanted to rest for any length of time.

And then she'd laughed. So easily. Twice. First, a stifled chuckle, and then a proper laugh. Without any concern.

And he was absolutely blinded by the sound.

*"GEN, GEN, GENNY," Oliver sang, searching for her and knowing exactly where she would be.*

*"You know I hate that name, Oliver Sinclair, you brute," Genevieve grouched in her little seven-year-old voice. She sat in her usual spot under the oak tree as he'd expected, leaning against it with her knees bent in front of her. She held a stack of parchment propped against them while she marked the top page with the piece of charcoal in her hand.*

*Genevieve talked to him so easily now. It had taken almost the full two years, but he'd slowly built up her trust in him. He was so proud of the little hellfire she sometimes let out. She was always so quiet, even still. Not timid, but observant. As if always wary, always sensing her environment. When he teased her, though, she let out that vibrant spark she normally kept safely hidden in the depths of her pitch black eyes.*

*"But it fits you so well. Little Gen, my gem," He plopped down next to her and peered over her shoulder at the page she focused on. "What are you doing?" he asked.*

"Trying to draw the lake," she answered in a stern voice.

"You're doing a fine job," he told her, admiring her attempt. It wasn't exactly great, but what she did at seven was better than anything he could produce at fourteen. He'd expect no less. His young friend was focused, talented, more than a little stubborn, and likely had the best tutors in the country.

"Do you think so?" she asked genuinely, tilting her head critically at the image she created.

"I would not say it if I didn't," he replied, admitting honestly, "It's better than anything I could do."

"That's because you lack talent."

She spoke with such seriousness that Oliver just stared at her in surprise for a full beat. Then he burst out laughing.

When he finally stopped, Genevieve was looking up at him with a little smile on her small face. She looked almost pleased with herself for making him laugh so hard.

"I suppose you're right," he agreed fondly.

"Would you like to try?" she asked, already pulling a clean sheet from her stack and handing him the pile and the charcoal. "The only way to learn and improve is by practice."

Even two years later, it still struck him how different she was from a normal child. Almost wise. Something she didn't deserve to have thrust upon her so unforgivably early in her life.

Feeling a tenderness for his young friend, he took what she offered him and tried to draw the lake.

Really, he did try.

Quiet moments passed as he focused intently on his subject, and Genevieve watched the product coming to life under his hand from beside him. He became so engrossed in the task that, at first, he didn't register the sound he heard to his left.

And then his hand paused in its movements.

He turned and met Genevieve's sparkling black eyes. Not believing it was really possible. He must have misheard. For two years, he'd never once heard what he thought he did just now, no matter how much he had tried to encourage and coax it out of her.

But before his shocked eyes, her quiet giggles burst into peals of laughter at his botched attempt at drawing.

And Oliver had never before heard a more heartwarming or beautiful sound in his life.

# CHAPTER 9

## GENEVIEVE

Genevieve sat at the old, upright piano in the Birmingham Estate drawing room. The keys taunted her while she stared outside the window at the midday sun. Usually, this room wrapped her in its comforting warmth, allowing her to compose and unburden herself as it soothed her with its deep red wallpaper, intricately carved dark wood furnishings and gold detail, and the heavy but balanced scent of spice and flowers. Today, however, the notes did not come to her. She was consumed with thoughts of the day before. Seeing Oliver for the first time in over seven years. Ignoring him at dinner. Keeping her head high. Stealing glances. Ignoring how her body traitorously reacted to him.

She wanted to compose. She knew the thoughts circling her needed a release. But as she slouched back in a most unladylike manner, she was incapable of grasping one. Maybe she didn't want to play. Maybe there were some things she felt from yesterday that didn't deserve to be immortalized through music. No, what she wanted to expel through the notes was her anger, her resentment. But even that, she could not stop at long enough to capture.

There was a soft knock on the large, beautifully carved door, and Genevieve, abandoning her frustrating endeavor, called, "Come in."

Amelia opened the door and took a single step into the room. "Am I interrupting you?" she asked.

"No," Genevieve sighed, standing from the piano bench. "I can't seem to find the music today."

"I see," Amelia said too knowingly. "I wanted to see if you'd like to take a cup of tea with me?"

"Of course," Genevieve replied, and she crossed the seating area to pull the cord by the fireplace as Amelia entered the room, shutting the door behind her. Her sister-in-law sat on the light brown couch that faced the lit fireplace, and Genevieve took a seat beside her.

"How did you enjoy last night?" Amelia's question was gentle, but her eyes were assessing as she observed Genevieve.

"It was pleasant." Genevieve registered how the words left her mouth through slightly gritted teeth. She looked away, taking a moment to fix her composure. She did not want to reveal how affected she was by a supposed stranger or very old acquaintance.

"Was it?" Amelia replied thoughtfully.

"How did you enjoy it?" Genevieve deflected, though she knew her sister-in-law well enough to know her purpose with this conversation would soon be revisited.

"Oh, I thought it was very nice," Amelia answered absent-mindedly.

"Did you like the new design Prudence showed you?" she stalled further.

"It was lovely. All of Prudence's designs are."

They were interrupted then by the arrival of their tea. Amelia gave the maid a small smile and word of thanks, asking after the young girl's mother, who'd recently fallen ill but was slowly recovering. Once they were left alone again, Amelia occupied herself with pouring two cups.

"Do you want to talk about it, Genevieve?" she finally inquired directly in a soft voice, passing Genevieve her tea.

"About what?" Genevieve hedged, taking the offered cup.

"Oliver Sinclair."

When Genevieve was silent, fixedly stirring her tea and taking a sip, Amelia continued. "You know him. There is something there. A history of some kind. It was clear in the way neither of you spoke a word to the other, and yet you both spent the entire evening stealing glances when you thought no one was looking."

Genevieve felt her cheeks heat, a decidedly rare occurrence for her. She could count on both hands the number of times she remembered blushing in her entire life. All of them related to the current subject of their discussion. She traced a finger along the delicate teal and floral design on the edge of her saucer, not answering. Silence. Her lifelong friend.

"I am here for you, Genevieve," Amelia said softly, reaching her free hand out to still and gently hold Genevieve's moving one. Amelia waited until Genevieve met her understanding gaze before continuing. "Whatever you want to share or don't want to share, I am here. You can talk to me about anything. I will always keep your confidence. From everyone, including your brother."

Genevieve swallowed, taking a deep, fortifying breath. She lifted her chin and nodded before speaking. "I knew him," she admitted. "A long, long time ago. When we were children, before Gideon returned. Oliver was my friend. My only friend. Or at least I thought he was." She looked away with a shrug, her hand still in her sister-in-law's soft grasp. "And then he left. That's all there is to it."

Amelia's hand squeezed hers in either comfort or encouragement, Genevieve did not know. "Is that so?" Amelia asked.

"Yes," Genevieve said stubbornly, determined to convince herself more so than Amelia.

"Is that why there is such tension between you now? Because he left?" she probed.

Genevieve took her hand back, lifting her tea for another sip. As she placed the cup back on its saucer, eyes following it, she answered, "He left me, did not write, and forgot all about me. I was here, alone, without him. And then he came back yesterday apparently under the assumption that none of that mattered. That just because *he* was unbothered, I should be, too. But that's not how friendship works. One person is not the center of everything. I mattered, too. And he left."

Her thoughts spewed out of her the way they had refused to when she'd sat at the piano. She met her sister-in-law's sympathetic and understanding gaze, and Genevieve was struck with an odd discomfort. She felt seen, far too deeply. The only person she'd allowed to see her that profoundly was the boy who had left her.

"I see," Amelia nodded, her unusually husky feminine voice soothing. "I can't imagine how much that hurt. I do wonder why you are so angry with him, though, when from what I understand, you never were with your brother's absence."

Genevieve shook her head, her hot rage rearing its very welcome head and once again guarding the fragile parts of her, even if the intelligent part of her mind recognized the very sound logic of Amelia's observation. Her righteous anger had her bypassing it, though. "He was my only companion, Amelia, my only solace for years. *Years.* You do not know what it was like for me with my father. Not even Gideon knows or understands. Only Oliver knew what my world was like. How hard it was for me to trust, and I chose to trust him. And he abandoned me. What's more, at that point, Gideon had only just returned. I did not know him or what he would be like. I was sure he would be another version of our father. I was terrified, and with Oliver gone, I was completely and utterly alone."

A heavy silence followed her words, Amelia clearly processing what Genevieve shared. Amelia didn't push her, even though Genevieve could start to sense tension, curiosity, and perhaps some shades of her own anger radiating off her sister-in-law. Genevieve deflected again from that far, far too personal topic, which she knew had pulled forth Amelia's emotions. There was only one soul that knew that truth, and she kept the focus on him, finishing her thoughts.

"He didn't hurt me, Amelia," Genevieve's voice was quiet, spent from her heated admissions and the unending fatigue of maintaining her guard, her secrets. "He annihilated me."

# CHAPTER 10

## OLIVER

Oliver did not want to see her. He didn't. He just wanted to go to the lake because he'd been gone for years, and he loved that lake. Yes, that was it, he told himself, feeling like a fool as he crossed the grass at the back of Sinclair Manor, the oak tree standing proud and tall ahead of him.

Of course, he was going there to see the lake. Because the lake reminded him of Genevieve. Because the two were one in the same for him. They were *home*.

He hadn't seen Genevieve for a week now. Since that dinner at Sinclair Manor the day he arrived. But she hadn't left his thoughts. Her bitterness, her passion, her beauty. She was resentful and ill-mannered. It followed perfectly that she had also grown so attractive. Unpleasant on the inside, mesmerizing on the outside. Even as he thought it, he didn't believe it, though. He knew she wasn't unpleasant. She was *hurt*.

But, truly, did she really have any right to be so dramatic about it? He'd been her friend. He left to become more than what he was. To become a man. As his mother had said, it was not his responsibility to stay for her, to combat her loneliness. He *had* to leave. He needed to be more than just the second son.

And yes, he needed to be someone a duke would not think twice about his family associating with. He had come back once he accomplished that, and the very first thing he had done was seek her out. How was he deserving of such animosity?

Coming up on the oak tree, he felt the first wave of disappointment not seeing that elegant silhouette of a woman seated at its base, where a little girl once spent most of her days. He kept walking, though, following through on his ridiculous mental conversation. He was here to see that damned lake.

Rounding the tree, he came to an abrupt halt. All his own bitter thoughts dissolving completely.

Genevieve was here. Floating contentedly on her back in the waters where he had first taught her to swim. He could see her eyes were closed as she basked in the feel of the sun. Her arms stroking so gently, she looked like she only meant to caress the water with her hands, not stay afloat.

Back when they swam together, neither of them had cared or even noticed how under dressed they were, swimming in their undergarments. They were children simply playing together. As he got a bit older, however, he stopped swimming with her because he no longer felt comfortable doing so. He knew she would still swim often without him. She had loved it from that very first moment she let go of his hand to move through the lake on her own. He had realized quite quickly why. For her, the water was another world. One she had never been in before, and one that was wholly separate from her reality. In the water, she was someone else. In the water, she had once told him…in the water, she was a fish. He understood the rest of it. She was a fish. Not a little girl that someone hurt.

Still under the branches of the oak tree, Oliver watched Genevieve floating peacefully and had no thoughts whatsoever of that little girl he'd taught to swim. No, right now, Oliver was only hyperaware of the dress laid out carefully alongside a sheet at the edge of the lake and exactly how little *the woman* in the water must be wearing. His cock twitched as he thought on it, standing there unmoving.

Shaking his head in an entirely useless attempt to clear it, he forced himself to step forward and cross the grass and flowers he'd once picked for her. He came to spend time at the lake, which was exactly what he was going to do. If she also *happened* to be in it, then that was no concern of his. It had absolutely nothing at all to do with being closer to her. Perhaps he could poke at the lady's cool indifference from the other night to see if some version of that spitfire still existed within her.

He stepped up to the lake right beside her dress and the sheet she'd brought to wrap around herself.

"Gen," he pitched his greeting low on instinct, taking on a seductive timbre he hadn't consciously thought to use.

Oliver had to bite back his laugh at how spectacularly Genevieve splashed in the water. One second, she floated serenely on her back, eyes closed; the next, she flailed about before quickly sinking down to her chin and covering herself with her arms.

"Oliver." The way she said his name, her eyes wide and unguarded for the first time since his return, it was almost like before. A reflex. A name she spoke more than her own. His heart skipped in answer. But a moment later, her expression turned fierce. "What on earth do you think you're doing? Leave."

"I see you're still trying to turn into a fish, little Gen," he ignored her.

"Don't call me that," she snapped, making him smirk.

"You know you always loved it," he teased.

"I did not. And for the love of God, turn around," she said, water lapping at her face as she kept herself as low as possible in its depths.

The lake was beautiful, though. Crystal clear. Her slim arms could only cover so much. And as Oliver's eyes trailed down of their own accord, he found that seeing only the teasing curve of her breasts was significantly more enticing than if he could see all of her.

He turned around. For equal parts of saving her the embarrassment as much as himself since his own body had started reacting uncontrollably to the sight of her. He needed a minute to calm the blood pounding through him and gathering below his waist before she, too, saw more than he wanted her to.

Oliver heard her soft strokes as she made her way back to land behind him.

"Thank you," she muttered a moment later, her tone begrudging. He took that to mean he could turn around, and he did so to find her with the sheet wrapped around her shoulders, clutched in one hand at the center of her chest.

"Still like to swim, then?" he asked.

"No, Oliver," she quipped, rolling her eyes. "I was trying to drown myself."

Those words were like flame to kindling.

*"That's not funny,"* he hissed at her, his arousal immediately forgotten in the face of his terrified anger.

She had no way of knowing how much he worried about her when she was little. About that very thing. She had been so sad. So alone. So hurt. So broken. And so very, very small. He took such care to build and keep their friendship for years because he did not want that little phantom of a child to do something permanent. Not that she'd ever said it, but sometimes... sometimes her heaviness felt too much for a person, let alone a small girl, to bear. So, he'd tried to help fortify her. Tried to take as much of the load upon himself as she was willing or able to give him. And always, always tried to make sure she knew she was not alone.

He saw the surprise flit over her face quickly at his vehemence before she recovered her disdain.

"What do you care, Oliver? You left me. It shouldn't matter one ounce to you what happens to me," she fumed.

Oliver felt his vision turn hazy as his blood started pounding through him for an entirely different reason. "Left you?" he tossed at her angrily. "What do you mean I *left* you, like some cast over bride. You were a *child*, Genevieve. I was growing up. I *needed* to grow up. To become my own man. You always knew I was going to travel. I did not *leave* you. I went to build myself. And you call *me* self-absorbed?"

"Yes," she sneered. The sheet fell from one of her shoulders as she must have loosened her grip, more intent on their argument than holding it in place. He noticed her chest moving rapidly as her own rage and adrenaline kicked up. "Yes, you are self-absorbed. Because you think you going off to become a man was the beginning and end of it. It wasn't. Yes, you went to build yourself. *And you left me.* Admit it, you coward. Act like the goddamn *man* you have apparently become, and *admit it.*"

Her voice was potent, controlled, and somehow even more erotic. The black hole of her eyes blazed and threatened to pull him into their depths. Her thin but plump lips pulled down just the slightest bit in the frown he'd seen on her so often as a child. The sheet and her wet hair clung to her skin, but she stood there like a queen, passing judgment and finding him wanting.

Shit. He wasn't sure what he wanted to do more. Toss her right back into the lake. Or kiss her senseless.

Then her gaze dropped to his lips, making the decision for him.

# CHAPTER 11

## GENEVIEVE

One second, they were breathing fire at each other; the next, Oliver had grabbed her by the shoulders and slammed his mouth against hers. His grip was hard on her, his beard rough against her skin, the warm cedar of his scent intoxicating.

Immediately, she pushed him away with a firm hand on his chest. They both panted from the passion of their hatred for one another. Then she saw his expression begin to shift to one of contrition, his anger or lust clearing, and she could not have that. Could not have that anger disappear from either of them. Could not face what would be left.

So, before he could utter a word taking back the kiss, she grabbed his overcoat with the hand not holding the sheet at her chest and yanked him back to her. Genevieve gripped his coat so hard, she half expected to hear it rip at the seams as she sealed her mouth against his and kissed him back.

The kiss was not sweet. No, it was punishing. She poured every ounce of her rage, her resentment, her loneliness into it. And when he shoved his tongue into her mouth, she assaulted it on instinct. Then he bit down hard on her bottom lip, and she growled in the back of her throat, her hand letting go of the sheet to reach up between them and shove her fingers into his hair. She pulled hard on the silky strands, letting him feel hints of pain, as she directed his mouth over her the way her body craved.

His touch was rough as he grabbed her waist and pulled her harshly against him before wrapping his hands around her back to hold her agonizingly close. The action set fire to her blood, and she felt her core melt and turn molten. She arched into him, her body naturally searching for friction, and she found it. She felt the hardness between his legs push up against her and a noise of pleasure leave him. The sound was so erotic, it made her body burn still hotter for him, but it also broke through her consciousness.

Genevieve drew his head back by his hair while she wrenched her own lips away from his.

If possible, they were panting even harder. Neither one of them spoke. Just stayed wrapped around each other. Genevieve stared into his bright, dark blue eyes, so close to the color of their lake, and couldn't read what she saw there. Nor could she even begin to decipher what she was feeling. She imagined whatever either was, they both likely mirrored each other.

Taking a breath, Oliver bent down slightly without moving away so his body still covered hers, and he lifted the sheet back into place from where it had fallen, wrapping it around her once more. He stepped back, and Genevieve replaced his hand to grip the covering between her oddly sensitive and heavy breasts.

She turned, bending down to pick up her dress where it still lay in the grass. She could feel his eyes blazing a trail along the side of her neck before she walked around him, back towards the safety of her home, where she could untangle whatever the hell just happened in private.

He didn't stop her. She did not want him to.

~

GENEVIEVE SAT CURLED up under the safe oak tree, her head tucked behind her bent knees, her arms wrapped tightly around them. It was as small as she could get while still leaving room to breathe. And she did breathe. She focused on inhaling past the sting in her nose. She didn't really need to fight too hard to resist crying. It was second nature at this point, as easy as breathing. Which she did. Inhale. Exhale.

She stared out over the grass towards the lake, feeling the strength of the tree at her back. Her eyes focused on the foxgloves and stayed there. She did not think. Not about anything except how very pretty those flowers were. She never really noticed how pretty before that day three years ago.

She wasn't sure how much time passed, but soon she heard his footsteps approaching behind her. Genevieve mildly wondered if she'd summoned him through the foxgloves somehow. Ridiculous.

"There's little Gen, my gem," he sing-songed in greeting as he so often did, only now his voice was different, a bit deeper. He was growing up. She had grown, too, but he was growing, growing. She wasn't sure she liked it. Soon, he'd be an adult, and he would go out on those adventures he talked about more and more. She wasn't sure how to convince him to stay, but she hoped he would somehow change his mind before the time actually came. For now, at least, he was still Oliver, and he was still here.

His feet stopped right beside her, but she couldn't force her eyes to leave the flowers. She tried, but it felt like her eyes had to stay on them. Had to focus on the pretty thing in this ugly world.

"Genny?" Oliver's playful tone changed, and he crouched down next to her. His hand clasped one of her arms gently and tried to unravel her. When she would not willingly open, he moved his hand to her back and ran it soothingly up and down her spine. "What happened?" His tone was serious. She found his word choice interest-

*ing. Not if something happened, or if she was okay. Like he already knew the answer to both.*

*She supposed he probably did. Who didn't know about her father? She heard the staff whispering. They tried to pretend everything was okay to Genevieve's face, and they did show her kindness. But they never intervened when he chose to berate her. For killing her mother. For driving her brother away. For being repulsive and ugly and stupid and useless. A murderer. A family destroyer. A burden and a menace that should have died. Nor did they intervene when his hatred overcame him and he lashed out, so disgusted by her face that he had to strike it.*

*Granted, it wasn't often. Most days, he just ignored her. Like she was not even there. But every few weeks, the words would come out. Every few months, the strikes.*

*Today, it was his words. He'd found her using the desk in his study while she tried to capture the likeness of the ink and quill resting there. He was going out for the day, and she had started soon after he left. She had not noticed how much time she spent on her task, the details of the drawing coming to life under her still developing hand. But she'd dawdled too long there. He returned and yelled obscenities at her for thinking she could enter his study. He, then, took the drawing she'd worked on for hours, tore it up, and tossed it violently into the fire.*

*She had come straight to her oak tree after the encounter and had not left since.*

*Perhaps he was right. Perhaps she should have died.*

*"You can talk to me, Genevieve," Oliver's gentle voice brought her back to him. "You can always talk to me, and I will always listen. I will always believe you."*

*She felt tears begin to gather in her eyes of their own volition, but they did not spill over. She wasn't as weak as that. She couldn't remember ever being as weak as that. She finally met his gaze and was struck by the worry and concern painting his features. His dark blue eyes, darker than the sky, were troubled. For her.*

*She lifted her chin from behind her knees to rest it atop them.*

*"Alright," she said, her voice quiet and enduring. Because she believed him, too.*

# CHAPTER 12

## OLIVER

For three days, Oliver had not been able to get that kiss out of his mind. It distracted him all day and occupied him all night. It was…incredible. The way she'd kissed, reckless and punishing, determined to dominate him. He'd been hard for the better part of the days since and struggled to keep himself under control.

*Fuck.*

Tonight, he had to see her. In front of others. The Birminghams had invited them for a final dinner before they departed for London in two days, where they would join the Season and launch Genevieve into Society.

His cravat felt too tight as he sat across from his mother in the carriage, and he resisted the urge to pull at it as they made the short trip to the Birmingham Estate. Staring out the window without noticing the passing scenery, Oliver was barely cognizant of how he bounced his knee anxiously. How was he going to spend the evening with her after *that kiss*?

"What is the matter, dear?" his mother asked, casting him an exasperated look.

"Nothing," he lied, not bothering to shift his gaze.

"Well, something is certainly bothering you. I do hope you won't act so on edge during dinner."

He sighed, dropping his head back against the seat and closing his eyes. She was exactly right. He was so torn when it came to Genevieve, he was completely on edge. She irritated him with her judgment and scathing remarks. She positively infuriated him with her insults and righteousness. But there was still that young boy inside him that wanted to comfort and heal her for all the pain she'd always had to endure, the pain from him just another item on that list.

And now, he had to contend with his biggest complication yet because not only did he find Genevieve attractive, he *wanted* her. Not just physically. It would never be just physical with Genevieve, the person he knew as well as he knew himself since childhood. No, he wanted the hellion of a woman that she'd grown into, that spark that used to be buried in her eyes now the burning trait of her personality. He wanted her fire and insults and scathing tone and all. A large part of him *admired* the resilient, confident, threatening woman she'd become.

All of that put him decidedly on edge.

Arriving at the Estate, he exited the carriage and helped his mother down. Taking her arm and leading her towards the door, he took a moment to admire the rich Estate. His family did well for themselves, and Sinclair Manor was not small by any stretch of the imagination, but for Oliver, it felt dwarfed by the Birmingham Estate. Genevieve's home was larger and grander, its deep history and prestige clear. It was opulent, impressive, and more than a little intimidating. Making their way inside, he was keenly aware of the grandeur and luxury around him with the dark woods, intricate detailing, expensive furnishings. The luxury that had surrounded Genevieve all her life.

He could never be enough for her. Even as rich as he was. He could never deserve her or give her the life she was accustomed to. She deserved to marry someone with both riches and a title. Someone of influence. Not someone like him. A common man who earned his wealth through trade.

They were led to the drawing room, and Oliver catalogued all the inherited wealth that surrounded him as he proceeded through the large entry hall. Stepping into the room, however, he didn't take in the vastness that was twice as large as their sizable drawing room at home. Finally, his mind abandoned the comparisons he had been detailing with growing misery to instead focus on the woman that plagued him since the moment he returned home.

Genevieve was a vision in pale pink. Her dark hair pinned up, exposing her long neck. She stood proudly with her sister-in-law beside the light brown couch where they had been sitting. The Duke of Birmingham stepped forward to greet Oliver's mother and escort her to a maroon armchair by the ladies, but Oliver found it difficult to move from where he was frozen just inside the door, separated from the group.

She looked like an angel, lit by the glow of the fireplace. Her jewels sparkling. Her expression the careful one of observation that was her crutch.

It was only an extra moment or two that passed, but it felt like hours that he stood there, completely under Genevieve's spell. Oliver quickly remembered himself with enough time to avoid making a spectacle, but he did not miss the Duchess of Birmingham's knowing appraisal as he greeted her.

The ladies resumed their seats, his mother taking the armchair on the other side of Genevieve, and he took up a spot standing beside his mother. The Duke of Birmingham stood opposite him, a hand resting absentmindedly on his wife's shoulder. Oliver noticed how the duchess lifted her own hand to hold his, and he was struck by the tenderness of the gesture. He almost felt envious of it. His eyes shot to Genevieve of their own accord.

"We were delighted to receive your invitation, Your Grace," his mother spoke to Genevieve's sister-in-law. "It was kind of you to think of us before you left for Town."

"How could we not?" the duchess replied, her sincerity ringing in each word. "We are so close here at home. We had to see you at least once more before we left for the next several months."

His mother smiled, shifting her attention to include Genevieve in the conversation. "Are you excited for your Season, Genevieve dear?"

"Very much so," Genevieve answered. "I am quite looking forward to forming new acquaintances. Perhaps gaining a few new friends."

Was that a jibe at him? She didn't look at him when she spoke, but he sensed her awareness and how she avoided his gaze. Much like the dinner at Sinclair Manor. Much like he was also trying to do now.

"You'll have wonderful fun," his mother agreed. "The balls, the parties, the dances, the suitors." Her voice was overly wistful, of course. "You will make plenty of acquaintances, I daresay, with your beauty. But I do hope you find some true friends. Young women can sometimes forget that we are and must be one another's greatest supports, and instead turn vicious in jealousy. Even over silly things. Like men."

"Oh, dear," Genevieve twisted her lip to the side.

It was adorable.

"Well, in any case," her brother cut in this time. "There is no reason to have too much fun or worry about gentlemen this year. It's only your first Season." His voice sounded a little tense, which piqued Oliver's interest, and he found himself in complete agreement with the duke.

"Darling, we cannot hold Genevieve back. It is her Season after all," the duchess spoke before focusing on Oliver. "Do you plan on attending, Mr. Sinclair?"

He hadn't known what to say as they all discussed Genevieve's coming out, his on edge feeling intensifying significantly as he thought of men courting her.

"I do not yet know, Your Grace," he answered truthfully.

"You must come, Sinclair," the duke's voice was strong and friendly. Oliver thought he might like the man. There was something similar about him and his sister, more than just their features, but Oliver couldn't place it. He also appreciated how clearly the duke seemed to care for and want to protect Genevieve. "We can share company with your brother, Charles, and my wife's brother, Thomas. It would be good fun for us, as well. What do you say?"

"Not too much fun, though," Genevieve sassed, and her brother pursed his lips at her in annoyance for being called out.

"Mother?" Oliver turned to her, unable to deny his immediate and eager excitement at the prospect of spending the next few months near Genevieve, who he tried to remind himself he severely disliked as an adult grown. At the same time, however, he did not want to abandon his mother to lonesome months in the country after only just returning to her. But of course, he needn't have worried.

"Oh, you must go, dear," she said with her usual flair and reading him with ease. "I am of the age where I quite enjoy my solitude, do not fret over that. And if I change my mind, I will join you and Charles in Town. No, all you need concern yourself with is bringing me home a daughter-in-law."

Again, his gaze pulled itself to Genevieve without permission and contentedly drowned in the heavy, black pools of her eyes that were now on him. Those eyes that were never the black of emptiness. They were the black that held everything. Everything, all at once.

Fuck.

# CHAPTER 13

## GENEVIEVE

Genevieve wasn't sure how the rest of the evening went. She was still reeling. From seeing Oliver. The memory of their kiss three days ago. The way his warm hands felt on her. The way his lips clashed with hers. She hadn't thought of much else since.

Well... that wasn't strictly true. In spite of herself and her own stubbornness, Amelia's observation had also been circling her mind just as relentlessly as the kiss. Perhaps even because of it. The question of why Genevieve judged Oliver's departure so harshly when she never had her own flesh and blood brother's. Even more considering she had always known Oliver planned to travel. He never made a secret of it. As much as she tried to hide from the truth, the unfairness of her behavior was becoming difficult to ignore.

And the music had finally started flowing out of her when she turned to the piano. Making music out of the feel of Oliver against her. The rage. The passion. The desire. The way she continued to burn for him, even days later. The confusion of her feelings and her own culpability.

And now he was coming to London alongside them.

She had been hoping for some peace away from here. From him. The peace that had eluded her for the past week and a half since Oliver's return. But it seemed it wasn't meant to be. He would be there. At every event, at every ball. If not in person, then in her thoughts because she knew she would be looking for him constantly.

"Genevieve," Gideon intruded into her reverie. "You're terribly quiet tonight. Is everything alright?"

She hadn't been paying attention to what Amelia and Prudence were talking about, but they quieted when Gideon voiced his question. They had retired to the drawing room a little while ago, and Gideon joined them since Oliver left for the evening after dinner. He'd reasoned he was excessively tired but that his mother should stay and take the carriage home, while he could walk.

Genevieve had felt a pang of disappointment at his departure and an overwhelming amount of annoyance that she would care or be anything but happy to see him leave. Since then, she'd sat in the armchair by the fire, staring into the flames, probably looking like a right sight to her companions.

"I am sorry," she angled towards the two ladies on the couch and Gideon in the armchair across from her, aware of how rude her posture must have been, too, blocking everyone out unintentionally. "I am lost to my own thoughts this evening."

"Is there anything in particular that has you preoccupied?" Prudence asked, her tone suggesting she had a guess.

Genevieve hoped she didn't. She knew Amelia has cottoned on already based on how she approached the conversation of Oliver last week during tea. It was unavoidable. Her sister-in-law wasn't one to miss these things, especially in those she cared about and knew well. But if Prudence also suspected the turmoil she felt with regard to Oliver, Genevieve would be mortified.

"Just nervous about the upcoming Season," Genevieve lied.

She looked to Amelia, "In fact, I think I should retire, sister. I don't seem to be much for company."

Amelia eyed her, her concern evident but gentle. "Of course, Genevieve. Sleep well."

Genevieve was glad to stand, and bidding goodnight to her brother and their guest, she left the room. As soon as the door shut behind her, she leaned against the finely carved wood for a moment, breathing out a sigh to expel her tension. Then she made her way across the hall towards the grand staircase.

As soon as she touched the ornate banister, however, a hand shot out and grabbed her, pulling her into the dark alcove behind the stairs. A moment later, her back was up against the wall, and she was overwhelmed by the scent of cedar as a large and familiar body encompassed her.

"Oliver," her voice came out breathless from the adrenaline coursing through her. "I thought you left."

"Of course, you did," it sounded like he rolled his eyes, but it was too dark for her to know for sure as her own eyes hadn't adjusted yet. Then she fully registered the position they were in. He was hovering over her, their chests almost touching as she breathed him in. His hand still held hers while the other was flat against the wall beside her head, blocking her way out. She was surrounded by him. His hard body dominating and seducing all her senses easily. Hidden from any wandering eyes, no one would find them unless they intentionally walked into the alcove the two of them occupied.

Having recovered from the surprise, her heart started racing for an entirely different reason.

"What the hell do you think you're doing?" She hoped she sounded angry to his ears, because to her own, her excitement and desire were abundantly clear. She wanted his mouth on hers again.

"I don't know," he replied, sounding like he was making the

admission more to himself than to her. As though he genuinely did not know what he was doing or why.

So, Genevieve decided to hell with it. He could spend his time trying to uncover the motives behind his actions. In the meantime, she had him alone and in private, his body pressed up against her, and she wanted to kiss him again.

Letting go of his hand, she grabbed the edges of Oliver's dinner jacket, which fit delightfully around the hard chest she could feel beneath her fingers, and she pulled him completely to her, lifting her face to capture his lips with her own.

Oliver didn't hesitate for even a single breath. Immediately, he flattened his body fully against her, removing the little space that remained between them, and deepened the kiss. He grabbed her hip, forcing them as flush as they could possibly be with only their clothes separating them. His short beard was rough against her skin, and she loved the delicious feel of it. It spurred her on further.

Genevieve moved one of her hands to the nape of his neck, and she squeezed her fingers hard. He rewarded her with a groan from deep within his chest as he ground his hips and his considerable length against the ache she felt in her own body. Her blood seared within her as her heart pounded uncontrollably and moisture pooled between her thighs.

She felt like an animal. An animal that wanted to devour him as she pushed against him with all her strength, pent up feelings, and overwhelming arousal. She switched their positions, shoving him back against the wall as she ravaged his mouth with her kiss. He met her, his hunger matching her own, as the hand freed from the wall reached up and grasped her breast, pinching her nipple hard through the silk fabric of her dress. His touch was painful and made her wild. She wanted it everywhere on her, untamed and bruising.

She ripped her mouth from his with a moan, and Oliver moved immediately to her jaw and kissed down the column of her neck. His other hand moved to her backside and grabbed roughly as his hips thrust against her again. Genevieve pulled at the silky strands of his hair to guide his mouth back to hers, kissing him and sinking her teeth into his lips.

But then, Oliver gripped her firmly with both hands and gently pushed her back, holding her barely a few inches away.

They stared at each other, her eyes having adjusted to the darkness. His expression was unreadable as surely as hers was, too. She was on fire for him. The fire of lust. The fire of hate. The fire of something more tender. She was his inferno and wanted them both to burn alive in the flames.

"Goodnight, little Gen," his rough silk voice was deeper with his arousal, and it made her want to bite him again.

"Goodnight, Oliver," she replied, her own voice husky. She turned around, breaking his hold on her, and proceeded back on her original course. She climbed up the stairs and made her way to the privacy of her bedroom, where she spent the rest of the night heated and aching for Oliver Sinclair.

And absolutely infuriated about it.

# CHAPTER 14

## OLIVER

*E*xactly two weeks from when he originally left London, Oliver returned to it. He'd spent the past four days since the dinner at the Birmingham Estate, where he'd decided to attend the London Season, packing and preparing. Climbing the steps to the front door of his family's Townhouse, Davies, Sinclair House's butler, opened the door before Oliver even reached the threshold.

"Good afternoon, Sir," Davies received him. "Welcome back."

"Davies," Oliver replied in greeting with a half smile, stepping into the house. "I'm sure you quite missed me these last weeks."

"Indeed, Sir, it will do your brother good to have you join him more permanently the next few months," Davies told him.

"Where is he?" Oliver asked, lingering in the brightly lit entryway.

"In the library," Davis answered, and Oliver started in that direction. "Shall I call for tea, Sir?" Davies asked after him as Oliver passed the hall table with its tasteful flower arrangement and white, decorative vase.

"No, that's quite alright, Davies. Thank you," he threw a smile over his shoulder at the man as he kept walking.

"Of course, Sir."

Oliver's long stride covered the rest of the entryway in a few steps, and after passing quickly through the study, he joined his brother in the library.

The room was calming with cream damask wallpaper and built in bookshelves. The overcast day was visible through the two large windows on one wall, and a fire crackled in the fireplace below the large landscape painting on the wall next to it. The furniture was in varying colors that somehow all matched, and the tables throughout the room were tastefully styled with adornments and stacks of books. It was a very easy room in which to pass the entire day, relaxing and reading, which was exactly what Charles seemed to be doing.

"Is this what you do all day?" Oliver said by way of greeting, observing his brother reclined across the entirety of one of the soft orange sofas. He had an arm draped across the back of the couch, a glass of amber liquid in hand, while the other held a book open. "Why can't you do this at the Manor?"

"I could," Charles said, returning back to his book after his head had automatically lifted at his brother's entry. "But I like the option of other things available to me here, even if I don't necessarily choose to do them."

Oliver scoffed. "And what options are unavailable to you in the country, Charles?" He walked over to the side table beside the far window and began pouring a drink for himself.

"Pretending I am not getting married," Charles replied flatly.

Both brothers were similar to each other in height and build. They were tall, broad, with strong, muscularly lean physiques. But where Oliver went after their father's side of the family with his brown hair, darker blue eyes, and bolder features, Charles favored their mother's side with blonde hair, baby blue eyes, and a fine quality to his masculine, clean-shaven face.

"What's so wrong with getting married?" Oliver asked, loosening his cravat as he made for the couch opposite his brother, drink in hand. He sat down, reclining comfortably with one ankle crossed over his knee. He leaned one arm on the armrest, holding his glass in his lap, while the other extended across the back of the couch. "You'd have to do it anyhow, and Lady Anna has always seemed like a sweet girl."

"I am sure she is," his brother muttered. "That does not mean I would have chosen to marry her if I wasn't forced to do so."

"You might have," Oliver argued. Granted, it was equally true that he might not have, if given the choice, but Charles *didn't* have a choice. Why rail against the idea when you were powerless to change it? Not that Charles was railing. He was exceptionally level-headed and responsible at all times, though the constant deep warmth he possessed did not always shine through clearly beneath his stoic civility. But he was, without doubt, the best man Oliver knew.

That was a big part of what drove Oliver. His mother had been close to the truth when she guessed at his reasons for leaving England for so many years, but she hadn't been precisely accurate. He wasn't running out from under Charles's shadow. He was trying to become someone that could stand *beside* his brother. Even when they were children, Charles was always the responsible, sensible, first-born son that would take over the family business and estate. He might look like their mother, but his disposition had always been like their strong and serious father. Oliver's disposition, on the other hand, took after their mother's...more relaxed nature. And having been born second, he was allowed to be more carefree. He had less responsibilities, less expectations made of him, save for those that he made for himself.

"Whether I would have or wouldn't have makes no difference. Father just wanted us connected to the title. He wanted his grandson to be the next Earl of Dunhill, and the current one wanted the influx of funds we bring to his estate."

"That's the spirit," Oliver raised his glass, his mockery thick in the gesture.

Charles sighed, finally turning his head from his book to look at his brother across the small table between them. "What about you?" he asked, lifting a brow as he deflected. "Going to find yourself a bride this Season? It would make Mother terribly happy. Her youngest son returns and then finds her a new daughter all within a few months."

"She said as much before she practically shoved me out the door," Oliver admitted drily.

Charles chuckled humorlessly. "Well, what of it? You know, Genevieve Edwards is coming out this Season. She's grown into quite a fine young lady while you were away, and she was particularly enamored with you before you left, wasn't she?"

"She was," Oliver nodded, trying to hide how his heart started pounding at the sound of Genevieve's name and what Charles was suggesting. "That's not the case anymore, though. She absolutely detests me."

"Ha, I doubt that very much," Charles brushed the idea aside. "She wouldn't have visited Mother almost every week for seven years straight if she wasn't still desperate to maintain her connection to you."

Oliver lifted his glass, taking a drink pensively. Could that be right? Is that why she stayed so close to his family while he was away? He shook himself mentally as he lowered the tumbler back to rest against his leg. Whether or not that was Genevieve's reasoning, it didn't matter in any case.

"She's the daughter of a duke, Charles," Oliver reminded him. "The sister of a duke. She cannot marry me."

Charles's blonde brows furrowed deeply. "Why the hell not? Our family has wealth, and you also made plenty of your own while you were away. We've known them for years, and you two have been friends for the better part of your lives. I think you'd be a perfect match for each other."

"Charles, she's elegant and refined and has grown up in a level of luxury that I could never provide, rich or not. That type of wealth is inherited and tied to England. I could never give her what she's used to."

With the way Charles was looking at him, you'd think he'd spoken in a different language. Oliver didn't know what else to say, so he met his brother's gaze, which seemed to be a mixture of shock, confusion, and disbelief.

Charles finally spoke, his voice a low murmur before he turned back to his book with a dismissive shake of his head. "I never before took you for such a fool."

# CHAPTER 15

## GENEVIEVE

Genevieve, Amelia, and Mrs. Potters waited in the Birmingham House drawing room, spending time with George and Guinevere until their guests arrived. The light blue walls were bright with the sunlight pouring in from the large, open-curtained windows, and Genevieve played soft music for the children at the piano. They'd been in London for a week now, during which time Genevieve had been presented, they'd settled into the house, and had begun accepting the invitations they received while sending out a few of their own. The first of which was this afternoon. Amelia had invited her sister, Lydia, and their friends, Anna Lucas and Emily Davenport, for tea. Then, this evening, they would all attend the Gardiner's Ball.

Amelia's sister was the first to arrive for tea with her two children in tow. The Countess of Coventry, Lydia Colbrook, was much like her sister, sweet, loving, and without judgment. They also bore a similar appearance, except Lydia's features were softer and her coloring lighter with blonde hair and blue eyes. All four cousins had been born back to back. Adelaide was only a few months older than George, and John a month older than Guinevere, who was the newest and youngest of their shared brood.

Lydia entered holding Adelaide's hand, followed by their nanny carrying baby John in her arms. Immediately, George and Adelaide ran to each other.

"One would think they have not seen each other in ages with the way they behave," Lydia rolled her eyes striding forward without pausing. She gave Amelia a kiss on the cheek when she stood up from the pale, embroidered couch before placing a kiss atop Guinevere's head in Amelia's arms. She, then, turned to similarly greet Genevieve, who joined them from the piano upon the group's entrance.

"In their short lives, I'm sure a few days certainly feels like it," Amelia replied.

After greeting and kissing all the children, their nannies took them to the nursery to play as their enthusiasm increased with each passing minute. Amelia was pulling the cord by the fireplace to call for their tea when their remaining two guests were shown to the drawing room, and within a few more minutes, they were all settled on the couches and armchairs with their teacups in hand.

Genevieve had been surprised to learn about her sister-in-law's friendship with Anna two years ago. Not because Anna wasn't delightful. She was sophisticated, polite, and inherently kind with lovely red hair, crystal blue eyes, and an ethereal beauty. But by an interesting coincidence, she also happened to be the same woman Oliver's bother, Charles, was set to wed once she turned twenty. They would be getting married later this year so she could begin managing Sinclair Manor by leading the Christmas Ball.

Where Anna was calm and tactful, while simultaneously always maintaining genuine warmth in her demeanor, her close friend, Emily, was bright, boisterous, and playful with a sparkling face, caramel eyes, and brown hair. Emily was beginning her third Season this year and seemed not to have a single care or worry at all about her prospects. Hers was the unique type of temperament where one could not help smiling, laughing, and being joyful just by being near her.

"So, let us see," Lydia wasted no time. "We have quite a few things to accomplish this Season. We need to find Emily's match, it's Genevieve's debut, and we have to start preparing for Anna's wedding. Where shall we begin?"

"Not me, please," Anna said, politely, taking a delicate sip of her tea.

Both Genevieve and Emily replied at once, "There."

Amelia and Lydia gave eerily similar laughs.

On an objective level, Anna was absolutely the place to begin. The relationship between Anna and Charles still had yet to thaw, not that they seemed to dislike each other exactly. No, rather, they both had maintained a neutral indifference towards one another and the prospect of their marriage, which had been agreed upon many years ago. Genevieve didn't know for sure how long ago the match had been made, just that it was decided for the major part of Anna's life. But now the time had come, and not only was the marriage inevitable, it was impending. They had to prepare both in things, but also in Anna's disposition towards it.

On a subjective level, though, Genevieve wanted to start with Anna because she did not want to discuss her Season or potential suitors. She still could not get the intimacy she shared with Oliver thus far out of her mind, try as she might. As the days passed, her agitation had only increased rather than cooled. She wouldn't be able to think of other suitors while consumed by thoughts of the man she hated. Hated, she reminded herself. She needed to hate him.

Although, with each passing day, Genevieve was having more and more trouble remembering *why* she hated him. Yes, she'd been hurt when he left, but it was becoming hard to remember why it had been selfish of him to have done so. Truly, Oliver had always been clear about his intentions to leave the country. He used to tell her about his plans and the different places he would visit and study. She would always listen quietly, sadly, but never vocalizing her wish for him to stay, hoping he simply *would*. And the more she thought of it – during meals, carriage rides, playing at the piano, in the dead of night right before she fell into heated dreams of him – the more she realized how unreasonable she was being.

Why should Oliver have stayed for her? He had every right to leave. Yes, he should have written. But she never begrudged her brother either his travel or lack of communication for her entire life before he came home. If she was being honest, Genevieve wasn't sure anymore if she was actually in the right.

"Anna, come now," of course, it was Emily's demonstrative way of speaking that pulled Genevieve from her own musings. It seemed the group had agreed that Anna was, indeed, the priority, thank goodness. "You and Charles have barely spent any time together. You do your obligatory dances, your families meet for their obligatory dinners, but you haven't really learned more than each other's names in all the years you've been betrothed. Your whole life, practically, and yet you've never actually courted."

"What need is there to court when the goal of any courtship has already been accomplished? We're getting married. There's nothing we can do about it." Anna was matter-of-fact, but Genevieve observed the slight flush of her cheeks. It was subtle, her unease unnoticeable in her unchanged posture and steady eye contact, but Genevieve saw it. The way she saw most things others did not.

"There's nothing you can do to break your engagement, yes," Amelia spoke in a gentle voice. "But there are things you can do to benefit your marriage."

"Like getting to know each other. Learning each other.

Liking each other," Lydia added, her voice holding a more soothing quality that seemed natural to her in a way it wasn't to anyone else Genevieve had ever met.

"*He* hasn't done anything," Anna answered, taking a sip of her tea. Genevieve noticed how she used that sip to cover up her urge to swallow.

That was it. They'd hit the crux of the situation, she'd wager. The others seemed to realize this, too, and Genevieve, struck by inspiration, was surprisingly the first to respond.

"Perhaps we can host them." She turned to Amelia, her voice and body language perked up at the idea. "We can have a small, intimate garden party for just our families. The four of us, Gideon, Thomas, Charles, his brother. The children." She hoped no one noticed how her voice changed slightly, her heart rate picking up, at the mention of Oliver.

Amelia's eyes narrowed very slightly at her, and Genevieve saw the smile twitching to break free on her sister-in-law's face.

"That's a wonderful idea," Emily exclaimed, holding her free hand against the center of her chest, perhaps in the useless effort to subdue her enthusiasm. "Could I bring my sister, Grace?"

# CHAPTER 16

## OLIVER

Oliver and Charles rode the carriage in a peculiar quiet, neither of them saying a word or even noticing the resounding silence in which they traveled. Oliver's leg would not stop bouncing. He sat with his elbow propped against the carriage door, his fist pushed up against his mouth. His eyes tracked their progress to the Gardiner's Ball out of the window. Even when they arrived and made their way inside, the men's preoccupied silence persisted.

Oliver was anxious. He had no idea what he was doing. Obviously, he was here to see Genevieve. To spend time with her. And the part of him that he was especially frustrated with wanted to stop her from spending time with anyone else. Dancing with them. Sharing that passionate hellfire with them.

He had absolutely no right to stop her, and he knew that. Why should he even want to, anyhow? Forget their different stations in life and how unsuitable a marriage partner he was for her, she had been nothing but rude to him since he returned.

Apart from the times she kissed him like she was trying to destroy him, and he was eager for her to do just that.

He shook the thoughts from his mind as he and Charles

approached Lord and Lady Gardiner. They greeted their hosts before entering the ornate, large ballroom. The room was full of the Season's revelers, dressed in expensive silks in the latest fashions. The room glowed in the light from hundreds of candles, bouncing off the gold trim and casting shadows in its intricate carvings. Tables were set up strategically throughout the room, piled high with refreshments and flowers.

"I need a drink," Charles finally muttered to him, promptly turning and beelining directly to the nearest one. Oliver nodded pointlessly. Charles had already walked away, and Oliver was more absorbed in searching the throng of people circulating the ballroom. He moved further into the room, and it took him more time than he would have liked before he finally found her.

Genevieve stood with two other young women, both of whom he recognized though he hadn't seen them for close to a decade. One was his soon-to-be sister-in-law, Anna Lucas, and the other was the friend she was rarely seen without, Emily Davenport. Oliver's eyes barely paused on the two women, however, before his gaze settled and stayed on the woman he would never outwardly admit he'd followed all the way to London.

She was glorious. The tallest of their group. Dressed in a dark lilac dress that hugged her slim figure almost indecently for the effect it was having on him. She was the image of grace and sophistication, her jewels catching the candlelight from between her artfully styled dark curls. He could spend the rest of the evening in this exact spot, just staring at her, and he would consider it an evening well spent.

Genevieve must have felt his eyes because she lifted her gaze and looked directly at him, like she knew he stood there. Those dark black eyes saw too much, saw everything. He would have sworn she could see the thoughts that had just been running through his mind.

Before he could do something monumentally stupid, such as

interact with her, he turned abruptly and shot straight for the terrace doors. Once outside, he took a deep breath of the cool night air before planting his hands wide on the balcony railing overlooking the dark garden and dropping his head.

What the hell was he doing?

"What the hell are you doing?" The sharp words perfectly mirroring his own thoughts jolted him around.

The demon woman stood there scowling at him. She had to be a demon, summoned directly from his own personal hell. What other explanation could there be for him wanting this woman, someone he didn't *want* to want, nor could he ever have?

He stared at her for another moment where she stood on the balcony, no more than two feet away from him, and then he laughed.

If anything, her scowl made her all the more attractive.

"What's so damned funny?" She watched him like he'd lost his mind, and maybe he had.

So, he gave himself over to the madness and told her honestly, shaking his head as he continued to chuckle, "You are so beautiful, Genevieve."

Her scowl deepened considerably, and he laughed harder, matching it.

"You're making fun of me," she stated flatly, and he didn't miss the note of hurt in her voice. Because he knew this woman, *this woman*, as well as he knew himself. She was the other half of his life, whether either one of them liked it or not.

He sobered and stepped right up to her, his short strides eliminating the distance between them. Neither of them said anything as she watched him with those heavy eyes that carried the weight of the world within them, and he loved the feel of them resting on him. He reached up and curled his fingers under her chin, tilting it up while his thumb stroked her delicate jawline. He made sure not to touch her lips so she understood the sincerity of the words he said next was completely unrelated to the passion they shared.

"Not at all, little Gen," he spoke in a low, ardent voice. "My gem is the most beautiful thing that ever existed in this world. Always has been."

Her face showed no reaction, but neither did her words snap at him for using his full endearment for her. Something she had been doing if he even hinted at it since his return.

Her eyes, however, seemed to stare at him harder. As if she could search out any lie or ill-intent behind his words. More than that, though, he noticed how her breathing changed as her chest rose and fell almost choppily. He didn't quite understand it, but he didn't say anything. It was for her to process and decide what happened next. He waited patiently in the open evening air on the Gardiner's balcony, perfectly content to keep caressing her face as long as she'd let him.

Time began to move again. Genevieve took a deep breath, then raised her own hand to take hold of his. For a moment, it seemed like she simply held it after pulling it from her face, but then she let go and said quietly, "I should return to the ball."

She turned, and he watched her melt back into the mass of guests. He stayed there for a while longer, staring after her.

*Oliver sat in the roots of the oak tree, leaning against its base, the wind ruffling through his hair. He stared absentmindedly out over the grass to where he could see his home a short distance away. He held his diary detailing the plans of his future travels, all the things he would see and do, propped open against one of his bent knees. He'd been compiling his plans for as long as he could remember and wanted to make sure they were thorough. He turned back to his notes, flipping the page to review what he planned next.*

*He heard Genevieve's soft footsteps while he ran a finger down the list. Oliver tapped a particular line as an additional thought occurred to him, making a mental note to add it in when he returned home.*

*"Gen," he greeted distractedly when he saw her enter his periphery. She would know what he was up to. She'd seen this diary many, many times, listened to him talk about its contents and his ideas more often than he could possibly recall. Without a word, she sat down beside him and leaned her head against his shoulder.*

*That fast, she had his attention. Something was wrong. It was laughable how quickly his mind abandoned the planning he'd been absorbed in for the better part of the past hour. Now, he shut his book without a second thought.*

*"What's wrong, gem?" he asked, trying to cover his worry with gentleness as he placed the diary on the ground to his other side. He tilted his head down towards hers in an attempt to see her face, but she had it angled down, as if the weight she carried every day was crushing her.*

*He'd seen her like this before, and it was always when that bastard she had for a father said or did something to her. He could count on one hand, though, the number of times she'd leaned on him like this.*

*Genevieve had hinted at some of the things her father said to her over the years, struggling between the trust she clearly had in him and fighting the wariness of people that had been carved into her by cruel hands in a cruel home.*

*But he'd told her he would always be there for her if she wanted to talk and that he would always believe her. And he would. He did believe her already, even without her ever sharing in any kind of detail. He hoped one day his friend, his gem, would find the faith in him to share the burden that lay heavy on her tiny shoulders.*

*They sat unmoving as the minutes ticked by. Genevieve didn't say anything, and Oliver was finding it more and more difficult to wait, his worry eating at him. But he could hear her breathing. Hear how deliberate it sounded with each inhale, each exhale. His heart broke for this child that had to breathe like that. In and out. In and out. Focused. Purposeful. Strong.*

*With a tender instinct, he touched his lips to her hair, refusing to add the urgency of his own worry to her impossible troubles. He would be the solid thing she could rest on while she breathed under her tree. Someone showing her love and gentleness when no one else in her world did.*

*She sat up at his soft kiss and looked at him. That serious, assessing look in her gaze as she tried to determine his intent, his sincerity.*

*But Oliver did not see that.*

*He saw the entire right side of her face red and inflamed, the bruise blooming under her eye accompanied by a cut.*

*As if someone had backhanded her. Wearing rings.*

*Oliver wasn't a violent boy. He had always been sweet and kind. Open and welcoming to everyone in equal measure. He'd fought with his brother on occasion, of course, but that had been some years ago now.*

*But whenever he saw Genevieve – the sweet, quiet, resilient, strong, little girl – with a mark on her, with pain coloring her, he wanted to pay it back in kind. He wanted to give her father what was owed to him. A mark for each mark. A strike for each harsh word. A pain for each neglect.*

*While Oliver catalogued her face and tried to get a handle on his growing aggression, Genevieve had arrived at some sort of conclusion.*

*"I was practicing on the piano," she said, those six words more direct and open than any she had ever given him in past situations like this. "He shouldn't have heard. I was in the drawing room, and he was in his study on the other side of the Estate. I was practicing so quietly. I don't know how he heard." She looked off into the distance, shaking her head in her confusion.*

*"I should have just read or practiced my drawings in my room. Only... I could not help it," her mouth twisted, and she looked down at her fingers as if blaming them as she rubbed them together until they formed fists. "My fingers were itching for the keys. I had to play. And I*

thought he would not hear," she repeated quietly, more to herself than to Oliver.

He reached out and lightly unwound one of her fists to hold her small hand. She kept her gaze trained on where they were joined. He didn't say anything, only held her hand and watched her, his other arm resting atop his bent knee.

She still stared at their hands, but he noticed her chin tilt up slightly, drawing strength from him.

"He thundered into the room in an uproar, yelling about how much awful noise I was making, how unskilled I was, and how dare I torment him with my racket. And before I could even get up, he struck me, throwing me off the piano bench. I fell backwards onto the floor. For a moment, I had the mad thought that he was going to kick me then, but he just stormed out instead, telling me to shut up and stop torturing him with reminders of my existence."

She took a deep breath, as if exhaling the last of her story.

Oliver had never known rage like what he felt in that moment. He didn't know what to do with it, it was burning him up from the inside out. There was a roaring in his ears, and his eyesight felt blurry, maybe even red around the edges. He was going blind in his fury, picturing his sweet gem hit so hard she sprawled on the ground, bruised and bleeding. And in such a home that the natural thought when she was in a vulnerable position was that devil would take advantage of it to inflict yet more pain.

He couldn't do anything, though. He knew that. Oliver was a sixteen-year-old boy. That man was the Duke of Birmingham. Oliver was powerless against him. Genevieve was powerless against him.

But there were other kinds of power.

Oliver wrapped both arms around Genevieve, pulling her to his chest, as he leaned back against the oak tree. They sat like that, in a cocoon of their own strength and friendship, until the sun started to set beyond the lake.

# CHAPTER 17

## GENEVIEVE

Genevieve pushed through the crowd of people towards one of the refreshment tables. She needed to compose herself, to just *breathe*, before rejoining Anna and Emily or socializing with anyone else. She couldn't get her heart rate under control or the shakiness that had settled within her. Something in her chest quivered so inexplicably, like she was shivering with cold or heaving with sobs, though neither was the case.

She clutched a glass of punch, her hand shaking as she brought it to her lips and took two large gulps before stopping and wiping her lips with the fingers of her other hand. She kept them there, the silk of her gloves cool against her skin, as Oliver's words continued to tear through her. The way he'd called her his gem, as he'd always done. Without the usual teasing, singing tone he used to rile her up and pull her out of herself when they were young. Now, he said it in his deep, silky voice, invoking it like a prayer. Then there was *what* he said, the way he'd called her beautiful. She felt like it was destroying her.

Because those words were everything. And she couldn't *control it*. Any of it. Nothing. Not even herself.

"Are you alright?" she heard his voice as he sidled up quietly beside her.

Straightening her shoulders, Genevieve lowered her hand from her face to join it with the other around her glass. She didn't look at him, keeping her eyes trained on the dancefloor.

She would not reveal how much he had affected her. She would not show weakness.

"I am perfectly well, Mr. Sinclair," she forced ice around her words, her mind, her heart.

He made a derisive noise in the back of his throat. "Is that right, *Lady Genevieve?*" The mockery laid thick in his voice. "Then I suppose you're *perfectly well* enough for a dance."

Finally, she turned her head towards him. Oliver was baiting her, she knew, and the way he looked at her in stubborn challenge proved it. He expected her to reject him.

The shakiness eased within her, giving way to the perpetual annoyance she felt towards him, and she welcomed the feeling with open arms. This, she could handle. This, she knew and understood. Even though she had accepted over these past weeks that her anger towards him was rather unwarranted and unjust. But damned if she would give him any type of satisfaction by doing exactly what he expected.

"I would be delighted," she answered with a saccharine smile, placing the crystal glass back on the table before facing him fully. Genevieve noticed a flash of surprise cross his features, which he quickly masked with amused civility.

He wasn't backing down either.

Oliver never did.

GENEVIEVE COUNTED *under her breath as she moved her feet the way the dancing instructor had shown her. The waltz felt simple, the steps easy to remember as she moved through them in time with the*

*numbers she muttered, but she felt choppy in her movements. The grass was now bent and flattened in the small circle she'd been practicing in under the branches of her oak tree.*

*"Ugh," she groaned before dropping to the ground flat on her back, arms and legs straight out. "Why is this so impossible?" she asked the leaves waving gently in the breeze above her.*

*Not long after, a face replaced them, smirking down at her. Oliver had been perfecting that tilt of his lips over the last few years, and now at newly seventeen, he seemed to have found an expression that worked. Even she felt a little nervous when he gave her that look. His face had slowly been growing awkwardly into a young man's, his features becoming bolder, whiskers coming in above his upper lip. He'd also started wearing his hair slightly longer and almost too carefree. Too carefree to seem anything but deliberate. But she still liked it.*

*She'd been fond of Oliver since the first day he'd approached her while she sat under this tree, her face stinging. She'd watched him throw rock after rock that day and had envied him so much in those moments. His freedom to be joyful, even if frustrated. And then when he'd decided to reach out to her, she felt...seen. Seen and maybe as though that was alright. It was still some time before she trusted his kindness to be real and not fleeting, but she had always liked him.*

*Now, though, as she was growing older and so was he, she was more aware of him being a boy and felt the crush building up within her.*

*Oliver brought her back to the present. "What are you doing, little Gen?" His deep blue eyes were sparkling with mischief as he stared down at her.*

*"Resting while begrudging the waltz," she informed him, not moving from her prone position.*

*"The waltz, eh?" he asked, his lips pulling up into a full grin. "What's wrong with it?"*

*She sat up with a huff, letting her legs remain extended straight out. He sank down next to her, bending his knees and resting his arms atop them.*

"Nothing, I suppose," she stared at her feet peeking out from the bottom of her dress, and she flexed them in circles as she spoke. "It's quite pretty actually, when people dance it. But I can't seem to look pretty while I practice."

"Well, that's obvious," he said, knowingly.

"I beg your pardon?" she demanded, pulling her shoulders back and lifting her chin as she turned to him abruptly in indignation.

He chuckled affectionately at her, making her feel all of her young nine, almost ten, years compared to his growing seventeen. "Nothing like that, my gem," he replied gently in a rare use of the nickname as an endearment rather than a playful taunt. "The waltz is danced with someone. You need a partner to lead."

"Oh," her ire sank down into defeat as her shoulders slumped, and she looked at the toes of her shoes once more.

"What about your tutor?" he asked.

"My father dismissed him," she told him, her voice dispassionate. "He said the expense was proving too costly and fruitless to spend on an ungraceful waste like me. And that he will likely have to pay someone to take me off his hands when the time comes, so why bother trying to learn how to trick them into marrying me with dancing? I would only end up driving away any man he managed to buy."

Oliver's posture became rigid beside her, and she felt the tension rolling off him. "Did he do anything else?"

"No," she answered honestly before trudging on and bringing the focus back to the main issue at hand, hoping to loosen his posture and dispel the anger she sensed simmering within him. It didn't frighten her. He was the only one who could never make her fearful, no matter what she felt coming from him. "I learned the steps, though. And the counting. I'm just not very good."

Oliver stood forcefully to his feet and looked down at her, holding out his hand. His anger was still there, but with it, she saw fierce determination in his ocean eyes. "I will teach you," he asserted.

She stared at him for a long moment. He was accustomed to her *silent scrutiny and let her take her time as he held his position, waiting for her hand.*

*"Are you sure?" she asked, her brows scrunched and a bit of hesitation in her voice. She did not want to embarrass him with her clumsy moves. But even as she asked, her hand already moved into his and she was standing up. Because she already knew the answer. She'd seen it written on his face and in the resoluteness of his eyes.*

*"Any man will be lucky to marry you, Gen," was all he replied as he pulled her into his embrace, taking up the position of the waltz. He placed his other hand on her back between her shoulder blades, while hers rested on his upper arm because she was still so small compared to him. He began to move, confidently taking her through the steps of the waltz, and she followed him so effortlessly, she was shocked. She hadn't even moved this easily with her instructor the few times they had met. But she guessed it made sense. She was far more comfortable with Oliver, and both of them were naturally attuned to each other after all these years.*

*He wasn't done speaking, though, his voice quiet and forceful. The steel of his sincerity and anger making the words hard and lifting her heart in tandem with the easy way they moved together.*

*"Men will line up in droves for you. They'll fall all over themselves to hear you speak a single word to them. They'll fight each other for a dance. They would pay a king's ransom for just a chance at your hand. Your father is a bitter and evil liar. He would never have to pay someone to marry you, nor are you or will you ever be a burden. You are graceful, you are sweet, you are funny and kind. You are my gem. And you can damn well dance exquisitely."*

# CHAPTER 18

## OLIVER

They moved together seamlessly. They always had. Since Oliver first started teaching her to dance, he and Genevieve moved like they knew each other. Trusted each other. Fit each other. It was even stronger now. Now that they were grown. Now that he'd had his hands on her. Felt her against him. Basked in the fire she kept fully trapped and tamed within herself. He could feel his blood pulsing through his veins, gathering below his waist as he pulled her almost indecently close, breathing in her jasmine scent. He wanted to kiss and lick from her fine jawline down to the base of her neck, where he could see her pulse matching his own in excitement.

Genevieve was overcome by him, too.

He spun her around the ballroom floor and used the excuse of their movements to pull her still closer.

"People are going to start talking, Mr. Sinclair," she said with forced politeness and slightly narrowed eyes, but he heard how her voice had grown huskier with desire the more her body pushed up against his. He felt how her hand on his shoulder clutched him harder, almost painfully, fighting the urge to pull him closer, too.

Fuck, he loved how rough her passion was. How dominating.

"For the love of God, stop calling me that," he spoke without thinking, too consumed by his arousal to reply with any semblance of wit. "You're being ridiculous. And let them talk. I don't care who talks or what they say right now."

Her eyebrows pulled up, giving him an incredulous look. "*I'm* being ridiculous?"

"Of course, you are. You have been since I returned. You can't seem to help it."

"And you've been the image of sense, have you?" she sneered, and he wanted to bite her.

"You're the one starting in with this 'Mr. Sinclair' nonsense," he scoffed disparagingly, even as his cock twitched in his breeches. "As if you haven't known me your entire damned life."

She watched him for a full moment before speaking. "I haven't known you my entire life," she reminded him. "I knew you for five years, then I never heard from you again until now. Not a letter. Not a word." Her voice lacked its previous hostility, but he could detect the hurt beneath it.

He hadn't written to her. It simply had not occurred to him as an option. He was young and excited and, yes, *selfish*. It wasn't that he had not thought of her. He remembered and missed the little girl that was his friend, and there had been plenty he kept track of to tell her when he returned home. But she was the Duke of Birmingham's sister by then, and he merely assumed that she should not be receiving letters from a friend that was, by all considerations, nobody. He never accounted for the impression his silence would leave her with, though, especially since she had not arrived at the same conclusion regarding the appropriateness of his correspondence.

She was right. He *had* been self-absorbed.

The song ended, but neither one of them moved away,

agreeing without words to dance the next one, too. They were not done yet.

Oliver lost himself in her black eyes, and he saw the deep pain she still harbored from his absence, from his silence. She must have thought he'd completely abandoned her.

Hadn't he? Not intentionally or knowingly. He was just a foolish boy. But this woman remembered. And she was right. He might have been a foolish boy doing what he unilaterally thought right and necessary, but he could be a grown man now and take responsibility for his behavior. She'd trusted him after all. When she'd trusted no one else.

"I am sorry, Genevieve," he said softly. "Not for leaving. I needed to go. For me. So, I could grow and become the man I needed to be. Something more than just the Sinclair spare. Someone that could hold company with a duke's family. With *you*. I hope you can understand that. I *need* you to understand that. I never meant to leave you, nor did I ever want to. I thought of you often and missed you every single day. But you are right, I was a selfish child and only thought about what I was feeling. What I thought was best. I had not considered what you might have been feeling as a result of my departure, and for that, I am deeply sorry. I am sorry I did not reach out. I am sorry I made you feel abandoned."

The music kept playing, their feet kept moving, but Genevieve watched him with the same intensity as she had when he first asked the tiny creature huddled at the foot of a tree her name. As if she was trying to decide if she should believe him. If she *could* believe him. If there was some sort of cost to his kindness, his friendship, his apology.

As they spun around the room, eventually he noticed her lips twitch gently as she swallowed, finally breaking away from scrutinizing him with her decision.

"I understand that you had to leave," she told him, accepting his apology.

Oliver tried to subdue his heart's instinct to soar with hope. They were finally taking a step forward.

"You do? That easily?" Disbelief and hope fought for dominance in his tone, and his fingers flexed against her back.

"Has our reunion been easy for you?" She arched a brow, her gaze still heavy, but she did not wait for his reply. "But yes, I do. I have spent much time these past weeks examining my prejudices, as well. The way I judged you so harshly when I never did my own flesh and blood. Gideon left for an entire decade and never wrote or sent word, yet I never begrudged him his travels. I would be a fool not to recognize the injustice of my own behavior. And perhaps I also needed to see it. What going off on your own would do for you. I am glad it served you well."

He could see the words still pained her, but she meant them. And that was enough. Both could be true. He needed to go, she understood that, but it still hurt her, and he regretted that.

The song ended, and this time, he removed his hand from her back, pulling hers instead into the crook of his elbow. Without thinking about what it would mean, about the eyes already on them, about her station and his, he led Genevieve out of the ballroom.

She didn't say a word or ask questions, and Oliver was fairly confident it was because she knew exactly what he was doing. She likely felt the same need coursing through her as he did. Passing the other guests, he moved farther down the elegant hallway until he finally found a secluded room. Looking over his shoulder to ensure there were no witnesses hanging about, watching them, he whisked her inside.

Before the door could fully shut, Genevieve had him pinned against it, her hands planted firmly on his chest, as her lips claimed his in a rough and wild kiss.

# CHAPTER 19

## GENEVIEVE

It wasn't anger or frustration possessing Genevieve as she kissed Oliver, not that it had ever really been as simple as that. She'd tried to convince herself it was, but of course, there was the heated attraction she felt for the gorgeous man Oliver had become, feeding her anger in a vicious cycle that fed the attraction right back. No, the biggest thing she'd tried to deny were the tender feelings driving her to get as close to Oliver as it was possible for one human to be to another.

This time, though, she could not ignore it. It wasn't ire raging through her. It was gratitude and love. Gratitude for his admission and his apology. She'd known for weeks now with increasing and undeniable certainty that she was judging Oliver too unjustly and harshly. But something within her still needed her feelings to be understood. To be acknowledged. To be seen. And Oliver had always been able to see her.

She was grateful to finally hear his reasons for leaving and not writing in his own words, even though she knew them and had been turning them over in her mind endlessly these past weeks. He always intended to travel, and it was his right to do so. She'd forced herself to accept it was *her* selfishness that had expected otherwise from him. But she also needed his apology. Not for the leaving, but for his impact. For the hurt it still caused her. For not writing to her. Truthfully, she hadn't even known until tonight that he missed her during his time away, but she was glad he had.

The type of love, however, was harder to understand within herself. She did not know what kind it was, nor did she care as she lifted a hand up to the back of his neck and squeezed it with all her strength. The love she had as a child for her friend? The crush she had for the growing boy he had been? Something else? She wasn't sure. And when her action spurred Oliver's passion further, twisting them around to switch positions, crushing her body between the door and his hard one, she knew she did not care.

No, all she cared about as he bit her lip and she pulled his hair was the fire raging through her. Her dress was too tight. Her *skin* was too tight. Her fingers were sensitive and tingled with the urge to touch him everywhere all at once.

Her heart beat a rapid pace as he shifted his lips to her neck and began kissing his way down to her shoulder. Genevieve's breath came out in pants, and her core turned to liquid. She felt it gather in her center as her body started to ache for him, for what only he could give her. And when he flexed his hips, giving them both the delicious friction they craved like animals, she moaned from somewhere deep within.

"Fuck, I can't get enough of you," his voice was low and gravelly, and she felt it along her skin, raising goosebumps in its wake and adding to her arousal.

"So, take more," she replied in a challenge, knowing he would rise up to meet it, needing him to. "*Give* me more."

"Shit," his mouth was back on hers in a deep, searing kiss, and she ravaged him, her grip on his hair and shoulder hard. She wanted him closer. She wanted him everywhere.

Oliver started lifting up the skirts of her dress and gathering them at her waist. He pulled down her drawers, which fell to her ankles, and she quickly kicked them away. Then his hand found the place where she needed him most, and her head fell back against the wood behind her. "*Yes,*" she moaned when he slid his fingers along her folds, feeling how aroused she was for him.

"Fuck, you're so wet," he growled, moving his fingers to circle her clit. Her eyes rolled back before closing from the pleasure of his hand on her. She lowered one of her own to the hardness between his legs, grabbing and feeling the considerable size of him through his clothes as she caressed his full length.

"No," he said softly, prompting her to open her eyes. He shook his head as those deep blue eyes watched her with a combination of desire and wonder. The hand not teasing her momentarily dropped the skirts he held up to remove her hand from his body. He paused, keeping his grasp on her fingers in comfort so she understood it was not a rejection. "Not today, my gem. Today… today is for you."

Oliver pressed a finger inside her, keeping his eyes fixed to her face and watching every second of her reaction. Like he was desperate not to miss a single moan, a single breath. She didn't break the contact either, even as the sound that came from her was unholy. His mouth was on hers in a quick, punishing kiss before he broke it and fell to his knees before her. Letting go of her hand, he pushed her skirts up again and lifted one of her legs over his shoulder, opening her up for him as he dove beneath the layers.

Her breathing ricocheted. Oliver started teasing her bundle of nerves with soft, gentle licks while his finger pumped into her slowly and leisurely. For all their heated, fast, aggressive passion, he slowed himself down to a torturous pace. Because that's what he was doing, he was torturing her, driving her wild, pushing her to the place he wanted her. And Genevieve felt like a demon for him, possessed and blasphemous and *loving it.*

She used one hand to hold up the other side of her dress while she shoved her free hand into his hair, gripping it hard as she arched further into that sinful mouth.

He groaned deep within his chest at her crazed desperation. The sound and vibration against her spurred her closer to the edge she steadily climbed towards from his unhurried attentions. Her uncontrolled eagerness seemed to unleash him, ripping his control to shreds, as well. All his teasing was forgotten as he began devouring her with his mouth, licking, sucking, biting.

Her breathing became uncontained, her body started trembling violently around him as all her muscles grew taut. Her grip on his silky strands changed, shifting from owning him to holding on to him as she lost all her senses, her thoughts, herself. There was only him. Oliver. With his mouth on her, his finger inside her.

He added another, stretching and stroking in and out of her relentlessly. She bit her lip to keep from crying out at the intense pleasure of it, but she couldn't stop the loud moan he pulled from her.

Then, Oliver shifted his fingers, moving them within her to hit a spot deep inside, and she sucked in a harsh gasp. Genevieve stopped breathing altogether as she fought desperately to contain her screams. She was a shaking, quivering mess about to be torn apart. He was going to kill her. He was killing her. And she wanted to die.

Oliver pulled his mouth barely an inch from her body, looking up to lock his gaze on hers, his eyes full of hunger and lust. "Come on, Gen," he growled against her overly sensitive skin. "*Let go.*"

He immediately had his mouth back on her clit and bit with enough force to put the action just on the other side of gentleness. He kept his dark blue eyes latched to hers, unwilling to miss when she came apart.

With his fingers in her, his voice caressing her, his teeth biting her, and his eyes watching her, Genevieve shattered into a million pieces.

# CHAPTER 20

## OLIVER

Oliver reined in his horse in front of Birmingham House. The previous night at the Gardiner's Ball had been amazing. He'd been so anxious and stressed leading up to it, but once he was with Genevieve, he forgot about all the reasons he could not have her. It was easy to just forget everything, Society, expectations, his lack of suitability as a partner. When he was with her, he was just Oliver, and she was just Genevieve.

It had been the best night of his life. He couldn't remember a better one. Dancing with her. Talking to her. Finally clearing the air. And then the way she'd pushed him against that door. How she gave into her desires so completely, shamelessly taking what she needed from him without pause or apology. The way she tasted on his lips. The sounds she made as she lost all her well-kept control. It was the only thing he could think about today.

Last night, after a few more kisses, tender caresses, and righting themselves, they had rejoined the ball and the other guests. He'd needed the moments beforehand to calm his own body's raging reaction to the feel and taste of Genevieve. Once they were back in the ballroom, if anyone noticed they'd been missing, he could not tell. He was still consumed with watching her. She looked so loose and carefree after being with him, and the sight filled him with an overwhelming sense of male pride, knowing she felt that way because of him. That he could and did give her that.

Oliver hadn't been able to help himself, which seemed to be a recurring theme where Genevieve was concerned, when he asked her for a third dance.

So, now, he was here, climbing the steps of Birmingham House with the flowers he'd tucked gently into his horse's saddle during the ride over. He knocked on the door and was promptly shown into the large, open house that was brighter than its country counterpart. It was just as extravagant and lovely, but where the woods and warmth of the Birmingham Estate were dark and comforting, Birmingham House had more medium, neutral colors that balanced lightness with warmth.

He was shown to the empty drawing room, where he waited for Genevieve to be informed of her caller. Walking to the window, the flowers hanging from his hand, he looked out over Birmingham House's impressive garden with its sprawling flowers, large structures, and pathways made of greenery. The trees and shrubbery were arranged so deliberately that they formed a natural kind of maze and a contained, beautiful wildness.

"Oliver," Genevieve said his name with surprise, pulling his attention from the window to the drawing room door behind him. She stood just inside the doorway, dressed in her riding gear. The Duchess of Birmingham stepped around her into the room with an amused smile on her face.

"Mr. Sinclair," she greeted him as he crossed the room and approached them.

"Your Grace," he answered, bowing over her hand and giving it a light kiss.

"Let me call for some tea," she said politely, stepping away from him and towards the fireplace to pull the cord there.

Oliver's eyes found Genevieve again. She looked proud, sophisticated, and devastatingly sinful in her riding outfit. Her brow was furrowed in annoyed confusion as she observed him, and it made one side of his lips pull up in that smirk that tended to exasperate her when they were young. He wondered if it would still be the case all these years later. With all their bickering thus far, he had not yet had the opportunity to find out.

Genevieve rewarded him by pursing her lips, and Oliver wanted to laugh outright and kiss her. Not the fervent kisses they'd shared so far. Just a kiss. Because she was beautiful and sharp and funny. Because she was her.

The duchess had gone to sit by the window Oliver had just vacated, where she picked up a piece of embroidery he had not noticed sitting on the side table. She set to work over it, effectively giving them a semblance of privacy. But Genevieve still hadn't stepped fully into the room. So, Oliver decided to go to her, his strides swallowing up the distance between them in short order.

"What are you doing here?" she asked, trying to sound harsh in her words, but failing. It made him grin fully.

"I am calling on you," he said with mock patience, and she scowled at him, looking so much like the little girl he had known, his heart clenched. "For you," he lifted up the flowers.

She stared at what he offered her for a full minute. He didn't interrupt her as the seconds ticked by, only waited patiently for her to finish thinking through whatever was working its way in her mind. Then she looked up, her dark eyes meeting his.

He was shocked to find them glassy.

In all the years, through all the heaviness and pain, he'd never once seen her cry, and he could count on one hand the number of very few times she had almost looked like she wanted to. She'd always borne the weight of her life like a thing made of steel, refusing to crumble, even at the tender age of five.

"Thank you," she whispered and took the foxgloves from his hand.

# CHAPTER 21

## GENEVIEVE

"Are you going riding?" Oliver asked her, and Genevieve clutched onto the question like the life raft it was in the sea of her roiling emotions.

"Yes," she said, her voice coming out stronger. "My groom was just saddling my horse."

"May I join you?"

"If it is alright," she let the sentence hang in the air as she looked over his shoulder to where Amelia sat working on her stitching. Her sister-in-law looked up, meeting Genevieve's eye.

"Of course," she smiled warmly. "The groom may accompany you."

Oliver held out his arm. "Shall we?"

Within a few short minutes, they were off riding towards the park.

"Why are you calling on me, Oliver?" Genevieve finally asked the burning question as they rode side by side.

"I thought it was obvious," he glanced over at her from atop his horse. "We danced three dances last night. It would be improper if I did not."

Her heart sank a little bit. She had hoped he was calling on her in truth, but he was only acting for propriety's sake.

"I see," she managed to reply.

They entered the park and slowed their horses to a leisurely pace as they rode in silence for a time, the disappointment still weighing heavily on Genevieve.

"What happened after I left?" Oliver finally asked her, breaking the silence between them.

"Pardon?"

"When I left, all those years ago," he clarified. "What happened with you? What did you do for these seven years?"

She sighed, remembering. "Mostly, the same things," she told him. "Gideon had only just returned home before you left since our father had died. Do you remember? I don't believe you had the chance to meet him, though. There was only a very short time between his return and your departure."

"No, I hadn't," Oliver confirmed, pulling his horse to a standstill under an oak tree that reminded her of home. Stopping beside him, Genevieve wondered if he did so intentionally. To help her feel secure while she spoke.

"Well, I was afraid, if I am being honest," she looked out, unseeing, over the park, unwilling to meet his gaze so she could focus solely on her story. "I did not know Gideon, and I thought he would be just like our father. And then when you left, I don't know how to explain it properly.… It felt like the terror grew beyond what I could withstand. Not that you had any real power when it came to my father, but you had been there. And then you no longer were. I did not know if I could manage it on my own or if I even knew how to. I think that's a big part of why it was so hard for me when you returned. I still held that feeling of being utterly and inconceivably alone in the world. But I realize now that it was not your burden to bear. My loneliness was never your responsibility."

She paused, but Oliver didn't say anything. He knew there

was more, but of course he did, and he would not want to inter-rupt. Genevieve could feel his gaze burning a path along her skin, but she still didn't look at him.

Her voice was quieter when she admitted, "I think those first few months, I didn't speak at all to anyone, and it was almost two years before I spoke directly to Gideon. It probably scared him right out of his mind, but I could not see that at the time. It would have been difficult for an *adult* to see that, let alone a child. Anyhow, I eventually learned he was not our father. He was much, *much* different, and he bore many scars of his own. Mostly from our mother from what I could gather, though neither of us have ever spoken properly about our parents. She broke his ability to love, I think. I imagine it's part of why he left after she died. Even still, he found a way to love me. Actually, love me. And he showed it. It healed me somewhat. Him, too. But it wasn't until he met Amelia two years ago that he became… whole.

"I learned to trust him and his care. Amelia's, too, though more recently. I still played the piano, only more often since I no longer needed to hide my practicing. Gideon brought in a new governess for me, Mrs. Potters, who you've met. Someone he trusted to stand up for me, even to him, if she saw me hurt-ing. He let much of the staff go in those days, and I think it was because of me. Because they allowed whatever circumstances had caused my silence and fear, but how could they have stopped it? Regardless, you might remember how I loved music before you left, but in the years you were gone, it became so much a part of me. For some time now, I have been composing my own pieces. It became my center…."

She cut herself off abruptly, not wanting to finish the thought that almost escaped.

It became her center…when he was no longer there to occupy the space.

Their horses grazed as she spoke under the large oak tree.

Whether intentional or not, it *had* given her the security she needed to tell him about that time. She observed the couples she hadn't noticed while recounting her story promenade and picnic in the grass throughout the park.

"I would be honored if you'd play for me some time," he murmured warmly. She turned to look at him and saw the same kindness he often wore on his face as a child.

She had not known how he would respond to her words. She had forgiven him for his departure and meant it. She believed and accepted his apology. She also did understand why he left, recognizing she had no right to begrudge it, even if it still hurt. But she'd just shared with him the feelings the little girl in her had felt after his departure. It was not her intention to cause him pain by answering his question, but it was unavoidable. It was truth.

She didn't want them to live in the past anymore, though. In old hurts and childish resentments. So, she moved on.

"I wrote a piece for you," she told him. "After that day at our lake, when we first kissed. I could play it for you when we return, if you'd like."

He beamed at her then, excitement sparking in his dark blue eyes, and he looked so much like that twelve-year-old boy running excitedly to skip rocks at the lake that her breath caught in her chest. In answer, Oliver gently kicked his horse into a gallop back towards Birmingham House.

Genevieve laughed, following him.

# CHAPTER 22

## OLIVER

"The Sinclairs," Oliver heard someone call out as he and Charles entered the warm, candlelit gentleman's club. He followed the sound of the voice to see the Duke of Birmingham sitting, drink in hand and expression schooled in his usual cool indifference, next to his cheerful brother-in-law, Thomas Colbrook, the Earl of Coventry. It was the latter who had called to them across the smoke-filled room, and Oliver and Charles turned in unison towards the gentlemen.

After passing greetings all around, they joined the two men at their rather large table.

As they were served their drinks, Oliver could feel Gideon's curious gaze resting on him. Of course, the duke knew how Oliver had danced with his sister at the Gardiner's Ball and called on her the next day. He even walked Oliver out of Birmingham House, perfectly polite, after Genevieve had played that heart wrenching melody for him when they returned from their ride in the park.

Lifting the crystal tumbler to his lips to sip the dark liquid, Oliver didn't hear his companions' conversation as his mind went back four days to that afternoon. He had already felt emotionally twisted from what Genevieve told him in the park. He knew it would be difficult for her to share what it had been like when he left the country, and he also knew she had to tell him. And he needed to hear it. They had forgiven each other at the Gardiner's Ball, but they still needed to look the truth of what happened in the eye and share its burden. They could forgive each other, but if she was ever going to heal, if *they* were ever going to heal, she had to tell him. He had seen the tree in the park and known it would remind her of their tree at home, their lake, and make it easier for her to unload her burden, as well as for him to hear it and take on its weight. It destroyed him, picturing the young girl he'd left behind with such fear and loneliness.

Then, she told him about the piece she had composed and its inspiration. He had been overcome by his impatience to hear it immediately. As Oliver sat swirling the amber liquor in his glass at the gentleman's club, he didn't hear Charles and Thomas speaking next to him. Instead, he heard the notes of her haunting, powerful, joyous melody. It was pain, passion, pleasure, all in one, just like that first kiss. Everything he had felt, she fed it back to him through the beautiful music she created with her elegant fingers on those keys. She really was a gifted pianist. The best he'd ever heard, truly.

"Oliver," Gideon finally spoke to him, pulling him out of his trance. "You will be accompanying your brother this week, yes?"

Oliver looked up from where he'd been silently studying his glass for the past few minutes and blinked at the duke. He hadn't taken more than that first sip yet, thoroughly distracted by the memories of Genevieve.

"I am sorry, Your Grace –."

"Gideon," the Duke of Birmingham interrupted to correct him.

"Gideon," Oliver nodded, appreciating and feeling undeserving of the permission he had just been granted. "I was lost to my own wonderings. Where are we going this week?" He turned to his brother seated beside him in question.

Before Charles could answer, three men approached their table.

"Gentlemen," the one with the kindest face greeted them. He had blonde hair and blue eyes, and a dimple peeking through one side of his face as he smiled at the seated group.

"Philip, how good to see you, my friend," Thomas stood, shaking the man's hand. "Alexander, Jack," he nodded jovially, first to the man with dark hair, gray eyes, and an imposing presence, followed by their hazel eyed, brown haired companion, who returned the gesture with a polite smile on his face.

"St. Alsbrook," Gideon's tone was cold as he remained seated and didn't deign to look at the leader of the newcomers.

"Oh, come now, Gideon," Thomas said, rolling his eyes as he resumed his seat and indicated for their new companions to join them. "Philip only called on Amelia once. It's been two years. You have two children together. I think you can let it go."

Gideon glared at his brother-in-law, and Oliver's gaze moved between the men at the table. He didn't know half of them, and it seemed there was some type of unpleasant history between a different half.

"Apologies, introductions have not been made yet," Philip said in a cautious tone once the newcomers had been served their drinks. He turned to face the Sinclair brothers as he spoke, "I am Philip Mason, Viscount of St. Alsbrook. These are my friends, Alexander Vaughton, the Marquess of Ronan, and Jack Davenport." They nodded in greeting.

"It is a pleasure to make your acquaintance," Charles replied respectfully. "I am Charles Sinclair. My brother, Oliver," he waved a hand in Oliver's direction.

Oliver raised his glass, nodding once in acknowledgement. "An honor," he said, then took a drink, the liquor burning down his chest pleasantly.

"Likewise," Jack replied.

Jack Davenport seemed to Oliver a man equal parts sober civility and warm cheerfulness. The Viscount of St. Alsbrook, however, seemed the most charming and pleasant of the three, though not with the exceptionally merry temperament Thomas possessed.

The third man, the Marquess of Ronan, Oliver had heard of before. He was said to be a formidable man, but also a good one, taking great care in his responsibilities as a peer of the realm. Oliver could tell the marquess had an unyielding disposition. He could sense it emanating from him as they sat together in the gentleman's club, overriding even Gideon's presence. And that inherent type of nature had a tendency to intimidate people.

"So, what's all this about?" Oliver asked the obvious question. "What happened two years ago?"

Philip sighed. Gideon glared at him. Thomas rolled his eyes again. It seemed Alexander and Jack already knew the story as they relaxed, leaning back in their chairs and nursing their drinks. Charles, however, leaned forward with Oliver to hear the missing piece of this reunion.

"I made the decidedly foolish mistake of attempting to court the now Duchess of Birmingham," Philip told them.

"You wanted to marry her," Gideon corrected in a hard voice, his green eyes narrowed on the viscount with hostility.

"I wanted to *marry*," Philip returned. "I still do, though I do seem to have rather poor luck in that regard. Her Grace is a fine woman, which was my only reason for pursuing her for the remarkably brief time I did. She was not interested. She was in love with you even then and was nothing but civil with me. I am happy for her. And you, I might add, even if you are being completely unreasonable," the last he muttered into his glass before taking a swig.

There was a pause as Gideon appraised the other man in an

oddly similar way to Genevieve's quiet assessments. Finally, the duke relented with a muttered, "Fine," thrown in Philip's direction before he attended to his drink. It was clear he wasn't happy about being on good terms with the viscount who had pursued his wife, however shortly, but if he was anything like his sister, Oliver was sure the duke meant it. The whole sight of the interaction between the two men made Oliver want to laugh. He relaxed into his chair, his curiosity placated.

"So," Thomas exclaimed, looking around at them all and rubbing his hands together. "Can we get back to the original question before we found ourselves so off track? Oliver, Gideon wanted to know if you will be attending the garden party Amelia is hosting later this week. You are expected, as well, gentlemen." He nodded at Philip, Alexander, and Jack, and Gideon's expression darkened at his brother-in-law. It seemed the duke's understanding towards the viscount did not extend to inviting him near his wife, but he didn't backtrack on Thomas's courtesy.

"I believe your sisters will be in attendance, Davenport," Gideon added instead, then turned back to Oliver and prompted, "Oliver?"

"I would be delighted," Oliver answered, finishing his brandy. He had already planned to attend, and seeing Genevieve again was absolutely his sole purpose.

# CHAPTER 23

Genevieve stood with Amelia, Gideon, Lydia, Thomas, and Anna, as well as Philip Mason, the Viscount of St. Alsbrook, and Alexander Vaughton, the Marquess of Ronan. They made light conversation in Birmingham House's garden while they waited for the rest of their guests to arrive. Genevieve clutched her drink lightly in her hand while her eyes continuously strayed towards the Townhouse's back door, only partly listening to the passing pleasantries of her companions.

She heard earlier in the week that their party had grown slightly, expanding to include the viscount, the marquess, and by happy coincidence, Jack Davenport, Emily's elder brother, who would be arriving shortly with his sisters.

Smiling politely at a joke Thomas made, her eyes went back to the doorway to see a man and two ladies entering. Jack, Emily, and their younger sister, Grace, joined them. Genevieve had met Grace once or twice in the past. She was a few years younger than Emily, but taller, with light gold hair, a serious countenance, and an almost otherworldly beauty with hazel eyes that matched her brother's.

Gideon and Amelia welcomed the newcomers, and while

greetings passed around the group and footmen handed out refreshments, Genevieve's eyes were the first to see Oliver and Charles finally arrive, as well.

Joining the gathering, Oliver's ocean eyes kept finding hers whenever he paused in greeting their other companions. She took a cooling drink of her lemonade to calm the slight pounding of her heart. She would never admit it, but she had missed him.

"Could you two possibly be standing farther apart?" Emily's low, exasperated whisper had Genevieve's head snapping in her direction. Emily was looking at Oliver, and for a mortifying moment, Genevieve thought her friend saw what was between them. But then, Anna gave a delicate scoff, and she realized Emily had been speaking to her. Following Emily's gaze once more, Genevieve noted Charles standing beside his brother.

"The whole purpose of this gathering is for you two to start spending time together," Emily continued.

It seemed Amelia, arm wrapped around Gideon's on Anna's other side, was thinking the same now that all their guests were in attendance.

"I find myself in want of a walk, darling," she spoke to Gideon, but the plotting was so at odds with her honest, sweet sister-in-law that it lay thick atop her words. "Will you take me for a turn about the grounds?"

Gideon's expression was thoroughly amused as he smirked at his wife. Genevieve saw the laughter he fought to control twitching across his features and shining clear as day in the eyes he'd passed on to his daughter. He kissed her forehead in reply, and it was obvious to Genevieve that her brother did not trust himself to speak. Not that she blamed him. She was pressing her own lips together slightly, too, trying to contain her laughter at Amelia's transparency.

They began to turn away when Amelia executed the rest of her very obvious scheme.

"Oh, Anna, won't you join us? I do not believe you've seen the beauty our garden has to offer," and before Anna could reply, Amelia turned to her next victim, Charles. "You will, of course, escort her, won't you, Mr. Sinclair?"

Gideon was shaking his head ever so slightly as he squeezed his lips together, eyes on his wife as a few chuckles slipped past his control. Amelia, for her part, was either completely oblivious or completely uncaring of her husband's laughter as, having accomplished her plan, she simply turned around and began walking.

Genevieve sipped at her lemonade to hide her amusement from Anna and Charles, both of whom wore matching expressions of shock and embarrassment, their faces flushed. They were properly backed into a corner, however, and they knew it. It had been precisely Amelia's intent. Charles stepped forward and offered his arm to his fiancée without a word, and together they followed the duke and duchess.

As soon as they were far enough away, Genevieve and Emily caught each other's eye and broke out into peals of laughter, no longer able to contain themselves. They leaned on one another, instinctively holding their glasses a little off to the side so as not to ruin their dresses while they continued to giggle.

"Ladies," Lydia chided them, pointedly facing their other guests, in particular the viscount, marquess, and Mr. Davenport, who were new to their circle, but Lydia was clearly suppressing her own amusement from the way she rolled her lips together to subdue her smile.

Genevieve separated from her friend, the last vestiges of her snickering making its way out of her. Then her eyes instinctively found Oliver's deep blue ones, and she immediately sobered.

He was watching her with unrestrained adoration painted across his face. Like that was...*love* in his eyes.

"I do apologize, sirs," Lydia said, absentmindedly holding her husband's hand beside her. "We have been quite anxious to see our friend settled happily with her fiancée. Our joy momentarily overtook us."

"Not at all," the viscount replied kindly. "It is most understandable."

Lydia shifted focus to the youngest woman in their party standing across from her. "Grace, I must say, you are looking lovelier than ever, and you've grown so much. Will you be coming out soon?"

"Thank you, My Lady," Grace said, her voice delicate, sweet, yet proud. She stood straight, a perfect lady, her reserved demeanor the polar opposite of her rambunctious sister. "Next year will be my first Season."

"Oh, please, do call me, Lydia," the countess smiled kindly at her. "You must be excited."

"I am, My Lady. Lydia," she nodded, her face the picture of refined stoicism, which was especially surprising in one so young.

That's when Genevieve noticed the marquess. He was watching the young girl, his sharp, gray eyes narrowed curiously. He didn't move or speak, just held his glass in his hand and assessed her. Genevieve got the sense Grace could feel his gaze, but rather than quivering as Genevieve guessed most, if not everyone, did under the weight of the marquess's imposing presence, Grace stood tall, chin level, unfazed by the attentions.

"Lady Genevieve," Oliver pulled her attention from the marquess and the youngest Davenport sibling. He had moved to stand beside her and spoke quietly. "Would you like to accompany me in joining our siblings as they enjoy this magnificent garden?"

Emily, ever the keen vixen, stared unapologetically at her and Oliver as he spoke. Genevieve threw a scowl in her friend's direction, trying to convey to her to mind her own business, before she turned back to Oliver. She couldn't suppress the slight upturn of her lips as she looked up at his ruggedly handsome face.

"I would be delighted, Mr. Sinclair," Genevieve answered him, curling her hand around the firm muscles of his forearm, which she could feel under the rich fabric of his clothing. His cedarwood scent enveloped her as he led them away from the group and she fell into step beside him. They handed their glasses to a nearby footman before she followed Oliver into the built in natural privacy of Birmingham House's impressive garden.

# CHAPTER 24

## OLIVER

Oliver was in love with her. He had been for some time now. He'd likely known since his return. No, he *had* known, he just hadn't wanted to acknowledge it. But he was completely, thoroughly, undeniably in love with Genevieve Edwards. She was his whole damn heart.

The way she had laughed just now. He'd seen her laugh before, of course. It used to fill him with such pride whenever he made her smile or laugh. Hell, it still did. But seeing her now with friends, her brother and sister-in-law, carefree, surrounded by love, and giggling. It had taken all of Oliver's willpower not to fall at her feet and *just love her*. He didn't wait much longer before asking for her time and focused attention.

Now, he led her in the direction their brothers had gone into the Birmingham House garden, which was large and built to both impress and conceal. Her elegant hand with its long, pianist's fingers rested gently in the crook of his elbow, and he breathed in her jasmine scent as they walked.

"You are breathtaking, Gen," he said after a few steps, once they were out of earshot of their other companions. He watched her face, because he could not help it, and when she gave him a sidelong look, he registered her black gaze making a quick calculation. Then she tossed her eyes over her shoulder and ahead of them before moving her hand from his arm to grasp his fingers urgently and pull him off their current path.

After she dragged him through half a dozen turns in an increasingly confusing maze of large trees and shrubbery, he finally asked, "Where are we going?"

"Shh," was the only answer she gave him over her shoulder, and he couldn't resist chuckling as his heart pounded with excitement in his chest. It was another minute before she pulled him into a perfectly hidden alcove tucked surreptitiously into the greenery, which he would have completely missed had she not yanked him into it.

They faced each other in the small space, still holding hands, and he looked down at her. She was slightly out of breath, and her face was bright with excitement and activity. She looked *happy*. It was beautiful on her.

"There now," she said on a little laugh, and Oliver's heart swelled painfully. He swooped his head down, his free hand cupping her face, and kissed her gently to relieve the feelings demanding to break out of his chest. Her hand reached up and grasped his wrist, kissing him back.

Without removing their hold on each other, he pulled back and rested his forehead against hers. Oliver closed his eyes and confessed quietly, "I missed you, my gem."

She seemed so full of joy that it overflowed out of her in yet another happy laugh. She let go of both his hands in exchange for wrapping her arms around his shoulders and pulling him close. Oliver didn't hesitate. Not even for a blink of an eye. His arms encircled her waist and pulled her in, holding her body to his tightly. As tight as he could manage, burying his head in the crook of her neck. He inhaled the scent of her, the jasmine and notes that were inherently her and her alone underneath, letting the feel of her against every part of his body soothe the feelings overwhelming him.

"Why did you sneak me away, Genny?" His silent gem had still barely spoken to him, and while he loved basking in her joy, he wanted her voice. He had always wanted her voice. Since the first day he met her.

"I guess I missed you, too," she mumbled against his shoulder, embracing him closely. "And needed you all to myself. Besides, you are almost too handsome," she pulled back to look at him with mock anger. "How can I be held responsible for what you drive me to do with your rugged beauty?"

Oliver barked out a laugh. "Of course, how dare I?" he agreed. "Now that you have me and my *rugged beauty* all to yourself," he smirked at her, leaning down to brush his lips against hers as he purred, "what are you going to do with me?"

She sunk her teeth into his teasing bottom lip in response, lifting one of her hands from around the back of his shoulders to splay her fingers into his hair. She gripped him hard with her demand as she drove her tongue into his mouth in an unrelenting kiss. His cock immediately turned to granite as he responded in kind. His grip on her waist turned bruising as he pulled her against his length and returned her kiss with matching fervor.

Genevieve gasped when he thrust against her on instinct, and a moment later, her other hand lowered to his chest, gripping the fabric of his coat hard enough to leave wrinkles. She pulled him aggressively closer.

Oliver felt his control starting to slip. He loved this woman. He loved everything about her. And he wanted to make himself a part of her as surely and completely as she was a part of him. He knew he wasn't good enough for her, she deserved better than him. She always had. But he needed her. Desperately. Achingly. Heartbreakingly. Forever.

# CHAPTER 25

## GENEVIEVE

Genevieve felt so full of happiness, excitement, desire, and those impossibly powerful feelings she'd harbored in her heart for most of her life. And she poured every ounce of them into this kiss. Heat pooled in her core. Her body ached acutely for him, each passing day, each new kiss, each conversation with Oliver accumulating into a single, profound, heart pounding need within her.

She didn't have the words to tell him what he was to her. What he had been, what he was fast becoming. She did not even think she had the courage to admit it to herself, but she showed him. In the way her mouth moved against his. The way her hands clung to him. The way she held him against her as if there could be no space, nor would there ever be, between the two of them.

Oliver moved one of his hands from its punishing grip on her hips down to her backside, which he grabbed with enough strength to make her moan at the pain as he rubbed his gener- ous, exquisitely hard length against the part of her that was throbbing for him. The fire roared higher within her, and the heat intensified between her thighs. She sank her teeth into his lips again, completely uncontrolled. His answering groan made her shiver in his hands.

Their need was going to consume them both. And she was *desperate* for it to.

Driven by hunger and instinct, she released his coat and moved her hand lower still, wanting to feel him in her palm, learn the shape of him with her fingers. Her touch was cautious, wrapping around him as best she could with him trapped in the confines of his clothing. Oliver ripped his mouth from hers and moved his lips down to her neck, kissing her as she explored the feel of him. She tested her grip, squeezing a little more firmly, and the way he bit her shoulder made his pleasure clear. He shifted his hips, indicating what his body wanted, and she complied, moving her hand to stroke him firmly. With each of his gentle groans and panting breaths against her skin, her confidence grew.

Oliver seemed to forget himself completely as his lips came back to hers with an unhinged kind of urgency. He turned absolutely savage, and it *thrilled* her. One of his hands grasped her breast while the other ruined her hair. His touch was hard and harsh. He pinched her nipple roughly through her dress causing her to cry out and her blood to roar excitedly within her.

Genevieve released his hair to squeeze the back of his neck. Somewhere in the recesses of her mind, she registered that they were making a mess of each other. His clothes would be rumpled, her perfectly coifed hair undone. But she couldn't think of a reason as to why that mattered or why she cared. All she could think about was ripping into him and the feel of him ripping into her.

That was why, under the feel of his hands on her, the grip and stroke of hers on him, she did not immediately hear the sounds coming from behind her. Neither did Oliver. If they had, they likely still would not have been able to hide what they were doing, but at least they could have taken a moment to separate and compose themselves even slightly.

As it was, Genevieve still had her hand moving with growing eagerness against his length while he massaged her breast, their other hands gripping, touching, caressing, when the soft gasp behind her broke through their lust. Before they could move, Oliver was pulled roughly away from her. Genevieve was so brutally shocked out of their passion that she didn't even have time to react or make a sound before Gideon had Oliver turned around, her brother's arm cocked back, his intent clear.

He was unable to land the hit, though, before Charles, clearly registering the current situation much faster than either Genevieve or Oliver, was between the two men, hands up placatingly.

"Move Sinclair." Gideon didn't need to yell. The rage vibrating through his low words was more than enough.

"No, Your Grace," Charles replied, his tone simultaneously reasonable and understanding.

The women had moved to either side of Genevieve. Amelia wrapped an arm around her shoulders while Anna grasped her hand in comfort or solidarity, Genevieve neither knew nor cared. Her gaze fixed only on her brother, and she could not see or think of anything beyond it. Gideon's expression was cold and murderous, and it *terrified* her. His ire triggered something within her, and she no longer saw Gideon standing there, but their father. His anger. His hatred. His disdain. His violence. Her body began to shake uncontrollably, and she had no hope at all of ever finding her voice. She was frozen in terror.

"It's alright, Genevieve. Everything is going to be fine," Amelia whispered in her ear, feeling her tremble, but Genevieve couldn't hear her.

"He had his hands on my sister," Gideon seethed.

"I know, Your Grace," Charles agreed. "And he will do what honor demands, but this is not the way."

"He damn well will do what's demanded, or I will kill him," Gideon promised.

Genevieve's vision turned blurry as she hyperventilated. She couldn't calm her raging heart as it tried to break free of its cage in fear and anticipation of pain. She forced herself to inhale. Inhale, exhale. Inhale, exhale. Her vision cleared the smallest bit.

"*Gideon*," Amelia's voice snapped out like a whip, pulling everyone's focus, including Genevieve's, to her. Once her eyes were off the fury pouring out of Gideon, her mind remembered who he was. It was her brother. And her father was dead. Genevieve's breathing become a bit easier, her heart starting to slow down as reality came back to her.

Whatever passed between Amelia and Gideon in that moment, it did so without words, and it made Gideon glance at Genevieve. Confusion and concern flashed across her brother's face before he turned back to the Sinclair men with clenched teeth.

Genevieve's heart was still pounding too fast, but the fear began to recede as she fully returned to the present situation. Her eyes shifted to Oliver, and she noticed, with no small amount of relief, that he neither cowered nor suffered from the same terror she was experiencing in the face of Gideon's wrath. No, Oliver was watching her, his brows pulled down and ocean eyes drowning in worry. Genevieve could see his fists clenched as he fought against the urge to come to her. She wished he would, that he could. But she knew he could not.

It had been so long since she had been in that place of terror. So long not living under the constant threat of pain, both physical and not, that she was no longer equipped to handle her fear of it. She had become weak against it. Unprepared. Unsuspecting.

"You will come to the house tomorrow, Sinclair," Gideon's voice was glacial as he spoke to Oliver. "And you will make this right for my sister. I expect nothing less."

"Nor will you receive less, Your Grace," Charles was the one to continue answering. Oliver merely glanced at her brother and nodded.

"Fuck's sake," her brother sighed out aggressively, rubbing a hand down his face. "My name is Gideon."

# CHAPTER 26

## OLIVER

"Well," Charles said as soon as the carriage door closed and they were moving. "That was one way to go about it."

Oliver had his elbows propped on his knees as he leaned forward, head in his hands, fingers splayed through his hair. He sat across from his brother and could not believe how he had let this happen. It wasn't even getting caught in broad daylight in the Birmingham's garden, or that Genevieve would now be forced to marry him, although the guilt of that would surely come later, he knew. No, it was that fear he saw crippling Genevieve when her brother became violent in her defense. He hated that he had put her in a position where she experienced that. He could only imagine what memories that brought back, what instincts, and he *hated* it.

"Fuck," he ground out, squeezing his hair roughly before abruptly letting go and leaning back. He braced one elbow against the carriage door and rubbed his forehead with his fingers before lifting his head, pushing his fist against his mouth, and staring out the window.

"Oh, relax, it's fine," Charles reassured him from the seat

opposite. "You will agree to marry her, and all will be forgiven and forgotten once you two are wed."

Oliver could only shake his head, unable to formulate words to express the emotions barreling through him. Of course, he would marry her. He'd be *honored* to marry her. He would be the luckiest bastard in the world to marry her. But he'd still be the bastard that made her settle. That created a situation where she visibly trembled in fear when her engagement should have started with someone, *him*, down on his knee before her, promising her the world.

"*Fuck*," he repeated, once again dropping his forehead into the palm of his hand and closing his eyes.

"Why are you so upset?" Charles's voice held a note of accusation. "She's a wonderful young lady, and you were going to marry her anyway. Although, I wasn't anticipating such a *dramatic* approach to the whole thing. Still, you could do much, *much* worse than Genevieve Edwards. She will make a wonderful wife, and there wasn't going to ever be anyone else for you, Oliver."

"Of course, she will be a wonderful wife. There's *no one* better than her," Oliver lifted his head to glare at his brother. "But she deserved better than this. Than *me*. She shouldn't be forced to marry me."

"God, are you truly still on that?" Charles looked at him with such annoyed disbelief, Oliver turned away to look out the window once again. "That girl has been in love with you her whole life."

"She hated me just a few weeks ago," Oliver argued.

"She didn't hate you. She was angry with you because she *loved* you, you idiot," Charles's brows pulled together, and his face contorted like he was disgusted by Oliver's stupidity. "She's always fucking loved you, and you have always loved her. Sure, you both had to grow up a bit and that love had to grow up, too, but it was always there. She's your best fucking friend, Oliver.

And you're hers. She was never going to marry anyone else. There is no one, *no one*, that girl trusts the way she trusts you. And she *deserves* to marry the person she trusts most in the world. You are the only one, the only goddamn one, worthy of her. Start fucking act like it."

Oliver was quiet as he thought over the words Charles practically sneered at him. Watching the houses and people pass by on the street, he had to admit the truth within them. He was right that Genevieve deserved to trust her husband above all others. After what she suffered in her young life, how hard it was for her to trust, she deserved to have a marriage and a husband where that trust was easy for her. And whether he deserved her or not, that little girl had trusted him when she trusted no one. It had taken years, *years*, for her to do so. He knew, knew down to the marrow of his bones, that she would never trust anyone the way she trusted him. Even though he left. Even though they fought. Their trust was built over a lifetime. She did deserve to have that with the man her life was tied to. She deserved to have everything.

Charles was right about another thing, too. Genevieve *was* his best friend. Even if he'd been gone for seven years. Even if they had been angry with each other when he returned. Her friendship had been the single most important thing to him when he was a child. It had shaped him from the beginning. And he knew, of course he knew, it was the same for her. He may doubt his worthiness of her, but he could never doubt their trust, their friendship, their history.

Oliver might not have a title. He may only have money, love, trust, friendship, *himself* to offer her, but he would give her all of it. He would give her everything. And he would spend every single day of the rest of his life making her happy. It was an honor he could not believe was now actually his.

# CHAPTER 27

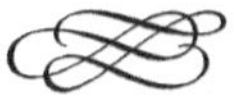

## GENEVIEVE

Genevieve sat in the drawing room of Birmingham House with Anna and Emily. Apart from the two of them and Lydia and Thomas, who were locked away with Amelia and Gideon in the study, all the guests had left. Genevieve battled a multitude of emotions, including guilt for sabotaging the whole purpose of today's party – giving Anna and Charles time together. But most of all, she was still recovering from the effects of that crippling terror she had felt in the garden. Not to mention the whole mess of things with Oliver.

Genevieve wasn't scared of Gideon, not at all, and she knew he was nothing, *nothing*, like their father. She had some guilt there, too, at the irrational, completely undeserving fear response she had to him earlier. He had never done anything to warrant such a reaction from her.

"Genevieve," Emily's usually bright voice was gentle. "Please don't worry. Everything really is going to be alright."

Emily sat on the pale tan armchair beside Genevieve, while Anna was still next to her on the matching embroidered couch they occupied. She hadn't left Genevieve's side since her walking party had found her and Oliver together. Once Emily joined them, she hadn't left either. They both held and sipped at the cups of tea in their hands, and they kept their bodies angled towards Genevieve, their concern evident. Genevieve's own cup, which she had yet to touch, still sat on the table.

"It is," Anna agreed from beside her. "Oliver is an honorable man. He will do the right thing."

Those words just made Genevieve feel worse. She knew Oliver better than anyone. She *knew* he was going to marry her. Of course, he was an honorable man. None of them had any idea how honorable and kind and good of a person he was. Had always been. She had no doubt he would marry her. And that perhaps upset her more than anything else out of everything currently troubling her.

"I know he will," Genevieve explained to them, her eyes fixed on where her cooling cup of tea sat, mocking her. "I feel awful that he is now forced to."

Emily scoffed loudly. "My dear, if the way he looked at you and spoke to you are any indication, I am certain nothing will make him happier."

Genevieve glanced up at her, reading her friend's face. Emily really meant it. Her own head started to shake in response when Anna added in her sensible, warm voice, "It's true, Genevieve. I saw the way he held you when we came upon you. Then the way he watched you when your brother was upset. As if he could not care less about His Grace's anger. It looked like it took every ounce of his effort not to comfort you instead. That man is very clearly in love with you."

Genevieve's gaze moved between her friends, unsure of what to say. They truly believed what they were telling her, she saw that, but she couldn't find it in herself to agree. How could he love her? He had been gone for years, and then they'd been so awful to each other when he returned. Yes, they had worked through the past, but even so, that kind of animosity is not exactly how people in love behave. She saw Gideon and Amelia.

Thomas and Lydia. They didn't hiss and claw at each other. Ever. There was passion between Oliver and her, yes. She was in love with him, yes. She knew that. Of course, she knew that. She'd known she was in love with him since she was eight years old and he had said those words to her. *I will always believe you.* Without her telling him anything. Without her asking for anything. He simply believed her. He always had. But none of that meant he loved her back.

She felt a lump form in her throat and her eyes start to sting. Her friends noticed, and Anna clasped Genevieve's hand in her lap and gave it a comforting squeeze. Emily leaned forward to pick up Genevieve's teacup from the table and hand it to her.

"Have a few sips," she instructed, resuming her seat once Genevieve took the offered cup from her. Anna released her hand so Genevieve could drink. She appreciated their considerations, but they needn't have bothered. They did not know how well-practiced Genevieve was in controlling her tears.

Just then, the door opened, and Amelia and Gideon joined them.

"Ladies, we have had your carriage pulled around," Gideon told Anna and Emily. "We apologize for the abrupt change of events today, but we are grateful for your discretion and your care for Genevieve. I am sure she is most appreciative, as well."

Her friends smiled at her with such kindness, Genevieve had never felt more thankful for their friendship. They set down their cups and stood, each of them giving her a kiss on the cheek in turn and saying goodbye with words of encouragement.

"I will walk you out," Amelia linked arms with Emily, who was closest to the door, and the three of them exited, shutting Genevieve in with her brother.

Without a word, Gideon took the seat Anna had vacated, and Genevieve was struck with fresh nerves. Not out of any kind of fear. Whatever irrational response had gripped her in the garden was long gone, but her brother had still found her in a scandalous situation that he now worked to get her out of. Of course, he would have some words for her.

A few moments passed in silence, during which Genevieve could not bring herself to meet the gaze she could feel on her face. She kept her eyes fixed on the delicate, floral design of her teacup instead.

"Tell me," Gideon finally spoke, his voice grave.

Genevieve suddenly appreciated the combined sense of her friends in giving her the tea because she now took another sip to fortify herself. Amelia did not return, and Genevieve realized she would not.

"I met Oliver when I was five –."

"Not that, Genevieve," Gideon brushed her story aside. "I do not need to know what's between you and the Sinclair boy unless you wish to tell me. You are obviously in love with each other. Amelia saw it back in the country and informed me we would see you two set together soon enough. What I want to know is what that bastard did to you that made you so afraid of me today."

Their father. After being back for eight years, Gideon was finally asking her about what she lived through with their father.

"It wasn't you," she admitted, shaking her head, eyes still downcast. "I could never be afraid of you. I just…I did not know it *was* you. It may not make sense, but…." She trailed off, not sure how she could properly explain that she had not known it was her brother there at all. That she had gone back somewhere, somewhere ten years ago, somewhere she hadn't been in a long time and no longer knew how, nor possessed the strength, to endure.

She continued to stare at the cup in her lap, trying to find the words, when Gideon's hand entered her field of vision to remove it and place it back on the table. He then pulled her into his arms and held her. She was surrounded by him. His warm spice scent. The comfort of her brother, the first adult that ever loved her, that ever cared for her.

She began shaking after a few moments of being tucked safely in his arms, though she wasn't sure what from. She wasn't afraid anymore.

Then, her overwhelmed brain caught up.

She wasn't shaking. She was *crying*. Once the realization hit, it overtook her, and she sobbed for the first time in her entire life. He held her, kissing the top of her head, stroking her hair, letting her break down against his chest.

Minutes, hours, years later, when she had released a lifetime's worth of tears and pain, he repeated in a gentle, agonized whisper, his arms still wrapped tightly around her, "Tell me, sister."

And so, she did.

# CHAPTER 28

## OLIVER

Oliver rode his horse to Birmingham House the next day. Dismounting and making his way to the door, he fully expected the Duke of Birmingham to start their conversation by landing the punch Charles had prevented the day before. Oliver didn't particularly care. He understood and respected Gideon's desire to protect his sister. What did he know or care about Oliver's history with her?

No, as he was shown inside and Lewis led the way to the study, Oliver was more preoccupied with looking around and hoping to see Genevieve. He wished he could talk to her, make sure she was okay, but to ask for an audience with her right now would be inappropriate. He felt a twinge of disappointment that he couldn't at least spot her anywhere before he was being announced to the Duke of Birmingham, and Lewis was exiting quietly, shutting the door behind him.

Oliver walked into the masculine, wood paneled study, with books on the wall to his one side, a fireplace on the wall opposite. Gideon and Amelia were both in the room directly in front of him. They stood by the window behind a large desk and had clearly been mid-conversation when they were interrupted.

Gideon stepped away from her and took a seat in the dark, leather chair facing Oliver. He gestured to the seat opposite him on the other side of the desk with a terse, "Sinclair."

"Your Graces," Oliver bowed his head while stepping forward to take the seat Gideon indicated.

Amelia smiled at him reassuringly over the duke's shoulder as he sat down. "I will leave you two to discuss matters," she said and moved towards the exit. Gideon's hand shot out and grabbed her wrist before she could move around the desk, effectively stopping her. He didn't say anything when she looked at him, but his eyes seemed to burn into hers. He was squeezing her wrist in a way that must have been painful, and as Oliver watched, the duchess melted in response. Her eyes glazed over and focused so entirely on her husband as if he was the only thing in the entire world. The moment was so personal, so intimate, that Oliver had to look away and give them their privacy.

He noticed Gideon pull her wrist to his lips in his periphery before letting go, and Amelia started moving again. Oliver turned back to meet Gideon's unimpressed green gaze. He heard the door click softly closed behind him before the duke began speaking.

"You're going to marry her." Gideon was nothing if not direct.

"Of course," Oliver answered. He sat straight backed and sure in his chair, head held high. Genevieve didn't deserve a cowering husband. She deserved someone who accepted her hand with pride. Someone who understood the full weight of what he received and strove to deserve it. "It would be my greatest honor," he told her brother honestly.

"Her dowry –."

"Is hers," Oliver interrupted, his voice firm. "Please discuss that with Genevieve directly."

Gideon narrowed his eyes, assessing him. Oliver didn't break the contact.

"You know what our father did to her?" Gideon finally asked.

Oliver had not expected that question, and he was sure the surprise was evident on his features before he quickly schooled them once more.

"I do," he nodded. "Though, I am happy to know you do, as well."

"Why would you think she'd keep it from me?" Gideon probed.

"It is not a matter of her keeping it from you. Genevieve has difficulty speaking about it," Oliver explained. "That she would tell you at all is a testament to how much she trusts you."

"She told me yesterday," Gideon confessed, sighing. His posture relaxed somewhat as he leaned back in his chair, his expression shifting to one of unfathomable guilt. "I had no idea. I knew our father was a bastard. A cruel and evil excuse for a human being. But he never revealed that side of himself to me. I did not know how deeply the venom ran within him. I wonder now what our mother must have suffered to become the shell she was, and I unknowingly left Genevieve in his hands for years. She was just a baby...." His voice drifted off. The sentiment was so reminiscent of Oliver's feelings of abandoning Genevieve that his own regret now reared its head.

Shit, she deserved so much better from the men in her life. He would die before he let her down again, he vowed.

"I imagine she would have shared a similar fate as our mother," Gideon continued slowly, eyeing him. "Had it not been for you. Thank you for taking care of her when I was not there."

Oliver looked the duke dead in the eye and told him in no uncertain terms, "I will always take care of her. And no one need ever thank me for it."

The duke's lips twitched upwards, and he finally seemed to

relax his shoulders fully. "Let me be clear, I do not like how you two went about this," his tone was serious, but then he revealed a genuine smile. "But I am relieved that she found a worthy husband whom she trusts so implicitly. I am proud to soon call you brother."

This time, Oliver could not even begin to hide his shock. The Duke of Birmingham thought him worthy of his sister. Worthy to be his family.

Perhaps Charles had been right. Perhaps he had been a damned fool all along to ever think otherwise. There had never been any other end for Genevieve or Oliver except each other.

# CHAPTER 29

## GENEVIEVE

Genevieve sat at the piano bench in the drawing room, staring at the keys, but she didn't touch them. She didn't know what to do with herself. Oliver was expected at any moment, and he would be forced to accept her hand in marriage. How could she possibly play anything when the guilt and shame of that coursed through her?

Amelia opened the door quietly and stepped inside, shutting it again behind her.

"Oliver is here," she informed her. Genevieve's heart started to race as she stared at her sister-in-law, who approached her and squeezed her shoulder gently.

"Stop your worrying. Everything will be fine."

"He's going to have to marry me," Genevieve said by way of explanation.

"Yes, and?" Amelia asked, looking down at her kindly.

"He should not be forced to marry me because of a moment of passion."

"Genevieve, the passion was there because you and Oliver are in love. We all saw there was something between you two," she replied. "You were both fairly obvious. Prudence and I even started planning the design for your wedding gown before we left the country. We have a few options to show you."

"You what?"

"Honestly, darling," Amelia chuckled, her soft brown eyes twinkling. "Nothing about this is unexpected. Well, that's not entirely true. We had expected a more formal proposal, but this works, too."

"It's a scandal," was all Genevieve could manage to say as she reeled from what Amelia told her.

Her gentle sister-in-law scoffed right in her face. "Oh, please," she said, already turning away towards her favorite seat by the window, where her embroidery waited on the side table. "If you think this is a scandal, you would have been positively beside yourself with how your own brother went about it. This is nothing."

Amelia picked up her current project and set about getting herself situated to her liking before taking up her needle. Genevieve watched her, not knowing what to say. She still didn't agree with Amelia that Oliver wasn't being forced, but the fact that it was expected was an interesting new piece of information.

"Play something," Amelia smiled at her. "I am sure Oliver would like to hear it before he leaves."

That inspired Genevieve, and she turned back to the piano. Resting her fingers on the keys this time, she took a deep breath and played.

She played and played until, finally, the door opened again sometime later and Gideon entered, followed by Oliver. She assumed she would not be allowed to see him today and was both glad and wildly unprepared. What did you say to the man who was now stuck with you for the rest of his life against his will?

"My dear," Gideon said across the room, looking at Amelia expectantly with his hand outstretched. Genevieve twisted on the piano bench to see Amelia, lips upturned, carefully putting her embroidery down before making her way over to Gideon.

Genevieve's eyes went back to Oliver, who stood next to her brother, watching her with an unreadable expression on his handsome face. Genevieve couldn't look away. Even when Gideon, his wife's hand now safely clasped in his, said, "We'll give you two a moment," and left them completely alone and unchaperoned.

As soon as the door clicked shut, Oliver was moving. Within a heartbeat, he was beside her, taking a seat on the bench with his back to the piano. He took hold of one of her hands, while his other cupped her cheek with a tenderness that made her heart ache.

"Are you alright?" he asked.

She stared at him, trying to understand what he was feeling, thinking, what he meant. She couldn't find an answer, just concern for her in his deep blue eyes.

"Yes," she answered him. "Are you?"

"I'm fine," he brushed the question aside. "I have never seen you react like that before, Gen." His hand left her face to grip her free one.

She swallowed, glancing away from the intensity of his gaze and the worry and fear there. Her eyes fixed on the light blue wallpaper as she started to speak. "I just…." She sighed, finally putting into words what happened. Because she knew, if anyone would understand, it was Oliver. "When my father was alive, I think I was always afraid. There was always pain and fear, at all times. So, I was…numbed to it in a way. It has been a very long time since I was in that place.

"When Gideon became so angry yesterday, I don't know what exactly happened. I could no longer see him there at all. I only saw my father and *his* anger. And it had been so long since I lived in or expected that pain that I did not have a guard against it. It just…terrified me." The last two words came out on the breath of an exhale, and with them, she turned back to look at him again.

His face shown with understanding and grief, and it healed something deep within her that even finally crying and sharing the past with Gideon had not been able to reach.

They stared at one another for what could have been minutes or hours, Genevieve did not know. She simply lost herself in the eyes that saw every deep, dark corner of her broken soul and accepted it from the very first.

Then, Oliver lifted both of her hands to his lips and kissed her knuckles softly. Without tearing his gaze from hers, her future husband lowered their joined hands to his chest, right next to his heart, and made his first vow to her.

"You will *never* have to be afraid again, my gem. Never."

And Genevieve believed him.

# CHAPTER 30

## OLIVER

Oliver was happier than he'd ever been in his life as he made the return journey to Sinclair House, and it was completely unexpected. When he left for Birmingham House that morning, the guilt still ate away at him, even as he carried the truth of Charles's words from the day before. But the duke's approval, even more considering the way he'd found Oliver and Genevieve in the garden yesterday, had done what all his years away had not fully accomplished. It eradicated the final kernels of self-doubt he still harbored within himself.

For the first time in his whole entire life, Oliver felt *worthy*. Worthy of Genevieve, her friendship, her love, her family. He was finally, *finally* more than the second son of a title-less house. Now, Oliver Sinclair was *Genevieve's husband*.

Oliver had a genuine spring in his step when he reached his family's Townhouse. Bounding up the stairs and through the door, he went looking for Charles to give him the recap of the day. Finding both the study and library empty, he went to the drawing room, where Charles and their mother sat on the sofas facing each other, the fireplace lit between them.

"Ah, my most errant son," his mother sighed fondly.

"Couldn't have done things simply, could you? Had to make a real show of it. Heaven only knows how you come by such a predilection towards the dramatic."

"Mother," Oliver stepped into the white walled room decorated with colorful paintings and furnishings. Stopping before her on the soft green couch, he bent down to kiss her cheek before seating himself on the other side of the matching couch Charles occupied. He relaxed, crossing his ankle over the opposite knee and leaning his elbow on the armrest as he began twisting his beard at the chin.

"Well?" Charles asked from beside him, his posture laid back, arm draped along the back of the seat.

"He did not punch me today either." Oliver knew that was his brother's first wondering, but the answer was also apparent on his unmarked face. "We will be getting married in two and a half weeks."

"And Genevieve?" his mother asked.

"Will also be there."

"Obviously," she rolled her eyes. "How is she?"

"Still shaken," Oliver confided. "It's not how it should have happened."

"No, it's not," his mother agreed, words sober for once.

"I think it was unavoidable, if I'm being honest," Charles murmured, and Oliver met his brother's clear blue gaze.

"What do you mean, dear?" their mother voiced the question.

Charles shook his head before giving a slight, exasperated sigh and addressing Oliver. "I think you blinded yourself with your insistence that she deserved a duke or marquess or some other ridiculous title. Your feelings, obviously, were clear as day to every single one of us, but you fought them. They were going to overcome you both one way or another. I think we're just lucky it happened yesterday with such a small, close party to know the tale, and only family members finding you."

"Finally considering Lady Anna family, are you?" Oliver smirked, snatching at the obvious subject.

"Anna was there?" his mother took to the bait immediately.

Charles's face hardened, which confused Oliver. Why was he still being so stubborn about the whole thing? And he called Oliver a fool, which of course, he had been, but how was Charles not recognizing the same sentiment in himself when he so sagely identified it in his younger brother?

"Yes, Mother," Charles nodded to her before turning back to Oliver. "Of course, she is family. She's my wife."

"Oh, how lovely you two are finally spending time together. I have tried, you know," she said, nodding and looking to Oliver. "While you were away, I tried hosting many a party, dinner, luncheon to get the two to begin forming a bond, but beyond the single obligatory dance or stroll, they would keep to their own sides of the room. It worried me," she told the last to Charles.

Oliver cleared his throat uncomfortably. "Well, I don't think they had any significant time together yesterday either. They were taking their first obligatory stroll, I suppose, when the party ended," he said with unnecessary discretion.

"Oh," and he'd never heard his mother sound so disappointed, but she recovered quickly. "Well, we shall have everything sorted with one of my daughters soon, and we can use the wedding festivities to resolve this issue with my elder one."

"There's nothing to resolve," Charles grit out.

"Tosh," their mother swiped a hand in the air in her eldest son's direction. Then she pointed at Oliver. "This one had the relationship, we just needed to take it through the last step. You, my firstborn, have had the final step decided for some time, but now we must get you the relationship. But worry not. We'll have you and Anna right sorted soon enough."

She said all this with complete and utter confidence, taking no regard of Charles's glower and Oliver's indecision between taking offense or being amused.

"Now, two and a half weeks, you say," she faced Oliver, who felt a flicker of unease at having her attention back on him and Genevieve. "I must meet with Her Grace to start planning." She stood and strode towards the door, as if she would leave for Birmingham House right this instant. Hell, for all Oliver knew, that was exactly her intent. "I will be sure to include both your wives," she called over her shoulder.

# CHAPTER 31

## GENEVIEVE

Genevieve waited with Gideon and Amelia in the park. She was so entirely preoccupied with watching for their companions to arrive that she did not bother pretending to listen to whatever her brother and sister-in-law conversed about.

It had been five days, five full, long days, since she had seen Oliver at Birmingham House. During that time, the wedding planning had commenced, Amelia and Prudence thinking of everything between the two of them. They included Genevieve and, to her happy surprise, Anna. Although, neither she nor Anna offered much. She had sensed Anna's unease, but Genevieve's own troubled feelings prevented her from asking after her friend.

The date had been set. The dress commissioned. The menu planned. The invitations sent. The Birmingham staff were well underway with their preparations. Everything was happening so fast, so terribly fast, and she had not seen Oliver through any of it. With each day, each new decision, each moment closer, she felt her feelings clawing at her inside.

She was marrying Oliver, the boy she loved, the man she

wanted, but he didn't really want her. He desired her. He would marry her because honor demanded it. But he didn't really *want* her, and now he was stuck with the little girl that had a crush on him. That punished him for leaving to become his own man.

He had been kind to her the other day. He was always kind to her because that was the core of who Oliver Sinclair was and always had been. He was the kindest person she had ever known. And she had no doubt he would be kind to her in their marriage. But she had robbed him of the chance to fall in love, to choose and marry his wife. Because she had to sneak him away in the garden that day. The garden in which both of their brothers were walking, but she was *so certain* their hiding spot was safe. All she'd thought about was being with Oliver, getting her hands on him, feeling his on her. She'd been so unforgivably mistaken. She had effectively trapped him.

For five days, Genevieve did little else but replay and replay and *replay* those thoughts. Each new wedding plan, regardless of Amelia and Prudence's excitement, adding fresh new fervor to them. Nor could she help the hatred she felt for herself and what she had done to the man she claimed to love.

Looking out over the park grounds, she tried to catch the first sight of carefree brown hair and a strong, bearded face. Instead, she found Anna headed in their direction, red hair glinting in the sunlight, accompanied by her parents. Seeing her eased Genevieve's current anxiety slightly now that her companion in misery once again joined her.

"Oh, Anna, how wonderful you made it," Amelia kissed her cheek before turning to her parents. "Lord and Lady Dunhill."

"Good afternoon, Amelia," Anna greeted her, then Gideon. "Your Grace." She then moved to Genevieve's side and murmured a greeting.

"How are you today?" Genevieve asked, resuming her search.

Anna sighed. "Charles is coming," she said by way of answer.

"Ah," Genevieve understood. In the back of her mind,

Genevieve knew that Anna's unease participating in the wedding planning was likely because her own future marriage was fast becoming present. That was also why Prudence determinedly included her at each step. Next, they would be turning to her wedding. "That's good. You need to spend time with him, Anna."

"It feels unnecessary," Anna said with a rare hint of petulance in her voice.

This time, Genevieve focused on her. "It is entirely necessary to spend time getting to know one's husband. How was it that day at the garden party? You didn't have much time together, which is yet another item on my list of many regrets. I am truly sorry for it. Tell me, how was the time you *did* have together?"

"You should not regret that," Anna's crystal blue eyes shone with sincerity. "Because of that moment, you will be my sister in our new house."

Genevieve reached over and gave Anna's hand a squeeze but did not respond otherwise, waiting for the answer to her question.

"We did not speak," Anna finally admitted.

"What?" Genevieve forgot her own worries in the flash of shock that struck her with Anna's words. She blinked twice as if her mind was trying to clear its vision and make sense of Anna's revelation. Genevieve's brow furrowed. "What do you mean, you did not speak?"

"Exactly that," Anna looked reflexively to the side as if catching movement, but Genevieve wasn't through with her.

"How could you not have spoken?"

"I don't know," Anna glanced back at her. "I guess neither of us had anything to say."

"God in heaven, Anna," Genevieve felt a wave of frustration, then she noticed what Anna had a moment before. Oliver, Charles, and Prudence walked towards them, only a few paces away.

Her heart spasmed at the sight of Oliver. He was so strikingly handsome. Possessing a wild sophistication. A confident grace. Those deep blue eyes were on her, and the nerves Anna had temporarily distracted her from rekindled in tandem with the heat only he could ignite within her. Still, she managed a low mutter to her soon-to-be sister before their final companions joined them fully.

"You damn well better speak to him today, or else I swear I shall tell Prudence."

# CHAPTER 32

## OLIVER

Oliver had to force his eyes from Genevieve as he and his family approached the waiting Birmingham and Dunhill party to greet the lot. He positioned himself beside her, however, and could smell the wisps of jasmine floating on the air.

He'd missed her this week. Hell, who was he kidding? Any day he was apart from her, he missed her. With each day, he could not believe his absolute dumb luck that Genevieve Edwards, this exquisite, elegant, breathtaking, sharp, fiery woman would be his wife. His goddamn wife. How the hell this had happened was beyond him, but he would spend the rest of his days thanking all manner of beings for it. Charles's logic and Gideon's approval had driven away the last vestiges of the doubt that plagued him, leaving behind disbelief and an unimaginable happiness in its wake.

"Shall we?" he offered his arm to Genevieve and followed Charles and Anna as they began to stroll around the park. He was impatient to be alone with her, to talk to her, to just be near her. He kept enough distance between them and his brother so they could keep their conversation private.

"How have you been, little Gen?" he smirked at her.

Her face was impassive as she answered, "Well. How are you?"

Oliver's brow pulled down. "What's wrong?"

"Nothing." Those black eyes glanced at him before facing forward again.

"*Something* is wrong."

She pursed her bow lips slightly, and he didn't miss how her fingers flexed against his forearm. What he wouldn't give to kiss her. They were in public, though. The next time he would touch her would be when they no longer had to sneak away or fear prying eyes. They wouldn't need to contain themselves or try to hold on to any kind of control. They could let go and finally fully unleash themselves on each other. The next time, when they started, they would finish.

He forced his thoughts to stop running rampant. Something was wrong, and he needed to stop thinking like an untried youth and take care of his future wife.

"Gen," he said, his tone serious.

"Did you know your brother and Anna do not speak?"

He understood her words as the distraction she intended. Oliver had never forced her to share anything before she was ready, and he would not start today. Even though his own worry was building up as he considered the possible reasons for her upset.

Really, there was only one. That while he had been spending the past five days blissfully imagining his life with Genevieve as his wife, she must have been dreading hers with Oliver as her husband.

He kept his voice calm, belying the sudden panic coursing through him. "What do you mean?" Oliver looked over at his brother and Anna up ahead and did, indeed, notice that they seemed to be walking in silence.

"Before you arrived, Anna confessed that she and Charles

had not spoken at all during their time together at the garden party. And it does not look like they're conversing much now, does it?"

"No, it does not," he conceded, trying to keep his main focus on their discussion rather than what troubled her and his assumptions around it. He wouldn't believe anything as truth until she spoke it, of course, but his guess was still there, starting to eat at the edges of his mind. "But you and I have other things to worry about instead of their marriage right now."

"Do we?" she asked nonchalantly.

Spotting a bench up ahead, Oliver altered their course, allowing Charles and Anna to proceed without them.

"Of course," he said, gesturing for Genevieve to take a seat before he sat down beside her. "Our own wedding is fast approaching. Perhaps we should focus on that before we concern ourselves with Charles and Anna."

"Your mother and Amelia have much of the planning in hand," she gazed out, nodding at a few acquaintances as they passed by their bench.

"And have you been participating?" he probed.

"Of course, but I have left most of the decisions to them." She finally met his gaze and held it, reading him. "I did make all the decisions for my dress, though. And Amelia and your mother also gave me a selection of embroidery designs they created for me to choose from. They assured me they will be able to stitch it in time between the two of them once the dressmaker finishes."

Genevieve's words had their intended impact. He was glad she was invested in the wedding, at least somewhat, and not totally sinking into herself with misery, leaving the planning and decisions to others. The reminder, as well, of how deeply the two of them knew and understood each other filled his chest with warmth, easing some of his panic, even though he still worried at what bothered her. Oliver would until she finally told him.

He couldn't stop himself from reaching his hand out where they sat angled towards each other on the bench and covering her clasped hands with his own. She moved one of hers on top of his so that she cradled it.

"I also demanded foxgloves for my bouquet," she told him quietly.

He looked up at her from where he'd been staring at their joined hands. "Did you, indeed?"

"Yes," she nodded, her black eyes penetrating.

Oliver smiled softly. "I am very glad to hear it. I have also been thinking – for our honeymoon, where would you like to go?"

Genevieve looked away, pensive for a moment, before her eyes alighted on him once again and she bit her bottom lip in hesitation.

"Can we go home?" she asked.

His face pulled in confusion for barely a second before he understood. A happy smile began to lift his lips. "Back to Sinclair Manor?" he asked.

"Yes," she nodded. "Just the two of us, while everyone else stays here to continue the Season? Only for a few weeks, of course. I am still quite concerned for Anna and Charles." She turned her head to where they could still see the pair walking in the distance. Oliver could not take his eyes from the wonder that was his wife. "Even if we must focus on us for the time being, of course," she finished, looking back at him, and he was thrilled to see a slight lift to the edge of her lips.

"I could not imagine anything that would make me happier," he told her honestly.

# CHAPTER 33

## GENEVIEVE

Genevieve watched the couples dancing around the Welsey's exceptionally large ballroom. The light from the many candles throughout the room sparkled and bounced off the jewels and finery of the circulating guests. Footmen prowled, offering refreshments that were also carefully arranged on tables against the practically golden walls. She did not want to be here. Oliver would arrive at any moment, and while she would like to see him, she also knew he was concerned about what worried her. He wouldn't push, but he was waiting, and she didn't have the nerve yet to tell him she was sorry for inadvertently forcing his hand. She did not want to have that conversation. She just wanted to go home. Back to the country, where she could forget all about London and the Season and all of this nonsense.

"My goodness, you are a brooding pair," Emily muttered, standing between Anna and Genevieve at the edge of the dancefloor. They'd been watching the many dancing couples silently for the past several minutes.

"What did you expect?" Genevieve turned to her friend. She

noted how lovely Emily looked tonight in a dark gold dress that brought out the bright honey of her eyes.

How no one had asked her to dance eluded Genevieve. No one had courted her yet either. Emily never gave a hint that it bothered her, but it must. And with her two friends now both to wed this year, Genevieve was sure it must upset her. She never said so or intimated any such feelings, showing nothing but unwavering support for them both, but Genevieve's worry was growing for her brilliant, starry friend.

"I expect you both to stop wallowing," Emily griped. She was right, of course. Anna and Genevieve were awful company at present, each of their sour moods the past week feeding and encouraging the other's.

"We are not wallowing," Anna spoke. "We are troubled."

"Why should you be?" Emily pushed. "Yes, both of your proposals were not what young girls dream of –."

"Neither one of us *had* proposals," Genevieve interrupted to remind her.

"But," Emily raised her voice slightly with the word, shooting her an annoyed glance, "you are both marrying two kind, strong, handsome, honorable men that will care for you. That are brothers, no less. Many women have had perfect dream proposals and not been so lucky in the men they were saddled with. Stop moping. Do something to ensure happy futures instead of focusing on whatever immense *troubles*," she rolled her eyes, exaggerating the word, "you both seem to bear."

Genevieve absorbed her words, not knowing how to reply.

Anna did, though. "It's not as easy as that," she said. "I do not know what type of husband Charles Sinclair will be."

"And whose fault is that?" Emily pushed, her tone shifting from tough love to gentle prodding. "We all know Charles is a good man. He will treat you well."

"I do know that," she nodded in agreement. "Or at least that he will not treat me poorly. But a lifetime of neglect and indifference can also be painful."

"He isn't neglecting you," Genevieve spoke up. "Or at least, he does not realize he is neglecting you, just as you do not realize you are actually neglecting him. I know you both well enough to say that you are each your own worst enemy right now. One of you has to ignite the change for it to take flame, Anna."

Anna expelled a deep breath. "I do know," she admitted. "I have been listening to what all of you have been saying, and I *have* heard you. It's just…difficult."

Genevieve nodded her understanding while Emily squeezed their friend's hand.

"What about you, Emily?" Genevieve turned to her. "We've *all* neglected you these past days with the commotion of my potential scandal." She widened her eyes on the last word in jest.

"What about me?" Emily asked, knowing exactly what Genevieve inquired after. "There's nothing to neglect or to tell. I have had exactly one dance so far this Season and no callers. I have officially assumed the role of wallflower on my journey straight towards spinsterhood."

"You will not be a spinster," Anna said so matter-of-factly and with such confidence, Genevieve had absolutely no doubt that she would see it through.

"You can't know that," Emily argued. She didn't sound bitter. Just sensibly resigned.

"I can, and I do."

Emily rolled her eyes again.

Anna pursed her lips at the gesture and continued, "Emily, you are handsome, well-bred, well-mannered, and have means. Two Seasons and a few weeks of another have not pushed you to the wall just yet. And you are, without doubt, the best of us."

Genevieve agreed wholeheartedly. They each had their strengths and gifts, of course, but Emily was brightness incarnate. If the feeling of love was ever made into a person, it would be someone like her. She was life and love and happiness. Men were attracted to allure and mystery, but all humans thrived and were sustained on the qualities Emily possessed in spades. Soon, someone would see it. Genevieve felt her resolve rallying behind Anna's newly revealed one. They would *make* people see it.

"That is simply not true," Emily scoffed.

Genevieve met her gaze, holding it to convey how deeply she meant the words she spoke next. "It most certainly is, Em."

# CHAPTER 34

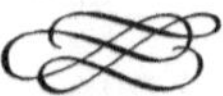

## OLIVER

"Ah, Misters Sinclair," Lord Welsey greeted them from beside his wife at the massive entrance to their ballroom. "How good of you to come."

"We are glad to be here," Charles answered graciously.

"We have received the invitation for your wedding, young Mr. Sinclair," the man grinned at him in such a way that Oliver felt his hackles rise. "Quite surprising. You have only just returned from abroad, the Season has barely begun, and this the young lady's first. Now, you are to wed the Duke of Birmingham's sister. In a matter of days, no less. There must be quite a story there," the gossipy old man fished.

"None that you would enjoy, Lord Welsey," Oliver ground out, forcing his voice to be courteous. "Said in such a manner, one would expect a rather scintillating tale, indeed, but the truth is far from it. My fiancée and I have been close friends since our childhood. Our courtship was not made in a matter of a rushed few days. It was built slowly and deeply over the past decade and a half. Lady Genevieve is a good and honorable woman, beyond reproach. To suggest otherwise would be most ill-advised." His words were civil, but the look Oliver drilled into the man and his tone made his threat clear.

Charles's hand came to rest on Oliver's shoulder. "As you can see, my brother is quite in love."

"How romantic, Mr. Sinclair," Lady Welsey said, seemingly genuine. "I did not know you and Lady Genevieve were such long friends."

"Yes," Oliver forced himself to unclench his jaw and reply to his hostess. "We are each other's oldest friends. We grew up beside one another."

"Oh, what a sweet story," she clasped her hands to her chest, her eyes dreamy, and Oliver felt himself relax. He quite agreed with her. "How lucky you both are," she continued, nodding to include Charles. "To have known your wives your entire lives almost. You will have such strong marriages that the rest of the *ton* will envy, no doubt."

Charles cleared his throat. "Yes, well, thank you, Lady Welsey. We mustn't keep you from your other guests any longer," he glanced pointedly behind him to those waiting to greet their hosts for the evening.

With that, the two men entered the ballroom. "He's a prick," Oliver muttered.

"And a loud one," Charles agreed darkly. "Any pot stirring he tries to do won't matter, though. His influence is nothing compared to Birmingham's."

"And Coventry's," Oliver agreed. He scanned the room while he spoke to his brother and found who he searched for standing in a sapphire blue dress across the dancefloor. Both she and Anna were clearly absorbed in a conversation that Emily did not seem to be agreeing with.

"You should dance with her," Oliver told his brother. He turned to find Charles's gaze fixed in the same direction as Oliver's.

"I will," he said, still staring.

"Why won't you two talk to one another?" Oliver asked his brother directly.

"What?" Charles glanced at him, his expression obviously trying to hide his guilt.

"You're both being so ridiculously stubborn, and for no other reason than what, pride? Discomfort? Insecurity? What is it?"

Charles shrugged, shaking his head, his eyes still on the young woman wrapped in olive green silk. "I'm not even sure, Oliver. I just know that when I am with her, I cannot find the words."

"The words for what?" Oliver pushed.

"*Anything*," Charles replied, frustrated, turning towards him fully. "Every other situation, I know exactly what to say. I am perfectly polite, tactful, diplomatic. But when I'm with her...." He trailed off, shaking his head again as he remembered. "It's not even that my tongue gets twisted, it's as if my mind has lost the ability to formulate words altogether."

"Do you think she's beautiful?" Oliver asked simply.

"What?" his brother pulled back, somewhat indignant, but obviously more embarrassed.

"Do. You," Oliver spoke each word slowly and distinctly, mocking his brother's idiotic reaction. "Think. She's. Beautiful?"

"Of course, I do," Charles answered, annoyed and blushing slightly.

"Say that, then," Oliver instructed, all notes of mockery gone. "Just remember these words and repeat them: 'You are beautiful, Anna.' Let her respond, *and then reply*." He said the last words forcefully so Charles didn't do anything stupid. "Do not shut down. *Make* your mind work. You are the most stubborn bastard I know. And a good man. Use that stubbornness to give your wife a happy marriage, even if you're unwilling to do so for yourself."

With that, Oliver slapped his brother on the back and went to claim his own wife's dances for the rest of the night.

# CHAPTER 35

## GENEVIEVE

Genevieve stared at her reflection in her bedroom's long, gilded mirror.

"Do you think along the neckline?" Amelia asked, head tilted behind her shoulder.

"The full bodice would look lovely," Prudence offered from her other side, both their faces assessing Genevieve's reflection with an artistic eye, deciding where to place their embroidery for the wedding in exactly one week.

Genevieve, however, was emotional. The dress, finished and fit to her long, slim frame, was perfect. Simple, yet elegant. No lace, no frills. Just shimmering, blush white silk that contrasted with her dark hair and dark eyes, and seemed to bring out the natural flush of her cheeks.

She loved it. She loved how she looked in it. How it hugged her hidden curves and accentuated her breasts. It was simultaneously tasteful and alluring.

She didn't want to make any changes to it. This was exactly what she wanted to wear, just as it was. Simple. Sophisticated. The wedding dress of Oliver Sinclair's wife.

"I don't want to change it," Genevieve voiced the thoughts

she had been processing for the last few minutes while her sister-in-law and Prudence busied themselves brainstorming behind her.

They both paused, their eyes finally lifting from the dress to look at her face in the mirror's reflection.

"You don't want any embroidery on it?" Amelia confirmed.

"Why ever not?" her flamboyant future mother-in-law asked.

"I feel like myself in this dress," Genevieve ran her palms along the silken fabric at her hips, admiring the feel of it against her skin. "Exactly how it is."

Amelia blinked and smiled warmly. "Well, then, that is a very good reason," she replied.

"It's too simple." Prudence wasn't as easily convinced.

"Though not boring," Amelia countered.

"But…." Prudence trailed off, her reflection deflating.

Genevieve's face pinched in confusion. There was something more going through Prudence's mind beyond the extravagance of the dress. She turned around and faced her.

"What's the matter?" she asked Oliver's mother.

"It's nothing," Prudence shook her head and smiled, but Genevieve only furrowed her brows, waiting silently. Prudence sighed. "You look lovely, dear, exactly as the dress is. And I want you to be happy with whatever you wear. I daresay, my son will be plenty pleased to see you walk down the aisle to him looking as you do now." She hesitated. "It's only that I wanted you, my daughter, to wear something I helped make for you. But those are the musings of a batty old woman and should not matter in your decision."

*Ah.*

The obviousness of what Prudence shared made Genevieve chuckle in disbelief for having missed it so thoroughly. The more she thought on it, the more Genevieve began to beam at her mother-in-law.

"Prudence –."

"*Mother*," Prudence's tone was that of a scolding parent, making Genevieve laugh as her chest continued to bubble with warmth.

"Mother," she amended. She reached out and clasped each of her mother-in-law's hands. "You are absolutely right. It had not occurred to me before, but I *do* want to wear something made by your hand and my sister's." At that, Genevieve released one of Prudence's hands to take Amelia's. "There would be no better way for me to walk down the aisle."

"My dear –," Prudence started, but Genevieve ignored her completely, not giving her the opportunity to insist otherwise.

Turning back around, she looked at her dress anew. "Now," she interrupted. "The challenge is maintaining the feel of Genevieve Sinclair while adding in the designs." Her head angled, eyes narrowing ever so slightly, as she took in the shape of the fabric and how it fell. She loved the elegant simplicity of it and didn't want any embroidery to take that away, but now that her mother-in-law had put the thought in her head, the dress felt visibly incomplete. Just *where* was the question.

Amelia walked around to stand beside the mirror and face Genevieve head on rather than assess her reflection. Suddenly, she breathed in a gasp and lifted sparkling, soft brown eyes to meet Genevieve's. "The hemline," was all she said, her voice low, almost reverent.

"*Yes*," Genevieve breathed, eyes widening before she looked at herself in the mirror again, her gaze falling to the bottom of her dress and taking in the length of her skirts.

She could see it. The hemline. That's why the neckline and bodice didn't feel right, it robbed the character of the dress. But the hemline would add understated charm to the dress. It would add family to a dress that matched Genevieve, matched Oliver, exactly as they were.

"We could run it all along the bottom here," Amelia moved around her, indicating her vision as she held up the bottom edge of the silk dress, "and trail it up, *only slightly*. So, the design is unobtrusive, unassuming, and entirely breathtaking. Perhaps a few tendrils reaching just above the height of your ankles. How would that look, Prudence?"

When Prudence didn't immediately respond, Amelia and Genevieve both abandoned the image they were creating to look up at her. Tears glittered in the strong-willed, colorful woman's eyes. When she felt their attention on her, she cleared her throat and nodded.

"Perfect for Genevieve Sinclair," she agreed.

# CHAPTER 36

OLIVER

Oliver held a book open in his lap, but his attention was fixed to the library fire before him. He sat in an armchair with his ankle crossed over his knee, his other hand holding the brandy he nursed.

Two nights. In two nights, they would finally be married, and he'd have his wife all to himself. He hadn't seen Genevieve since the Welsey's Ball over a week ago, and he was growing crankier by the day being separated from her. His mother insisted after their few public appearances as an engaged couple that they should now take the opportunity to let their hearts grow fonder. A load of horse shit, if you asked him, but what did he know?

He took another sip of his drink, remembering. Genevieve had been breathtaking at the Welsey's Ball. Hell, she was always breathtaking. He'd whisked her around that ballroom for hours, aware and uncaring of the eyes that tracked them. They'd gathered more than their fair share of attention since the invitations had gone out, and the *ton* kept a keen eye on the newly returned Sinclair son and the Duke of Birmingham's sister. They'd played their parts in turn. He didn't steal her away to a secluded room like the last time. Like he wanted to. They kept their conversations flowing and proper. Their smiles frequent and genuine.

Genevieve still hadn't shared what troubled her or let it show to the other guests, but he caught the unguarded moments where he could see the heaviness buried in her eyes. Oliver would have to ask her again. There was nothing else for it. He wouldn't push her if she still didn't want to tell him yet, but he didn't want their marriage to start with her bearing whatever burdened her alone. They would not be seeing each other again until they said their vows, but they had the whole carriage ride to the country to do nothing but talk. Well, nothing else until they talked.

"What are you doing?" Charles's voice shook him from his thoughts, and he turned around to see his older brother striding into the library and pouring himself a drink. Oliver had to blink a few times for his eyes to adjust after staring into the fire for so long.

He held up his book to answer Charles as the latter joined him in the adjacent armchair. "Reading," Oliver answered unnecessarily.

"Of course, you were," Charles replied with sarcasm. "What's on your mind? Wedding nerves?"

"No." Oliver placed the book on the small table between them. "Not at all, actually."

"Then?" his brother prompted, taking a swig of his liquor.

"Something is troubling Genevieve, and she hasn't told me what it is yet."

"Have you tried talking to her?"

Oliver gave Charles an exaggerated look. "I hope the irony of that question is not lost on you, brother."

Charles only scoffed in answer, eyes on the flames in the fireplace.

Taking a breath, Oliver moved his glass to cup it between both of his palms. "I have asked her, but she wasn't ready to discuss it yet. I plan to broach the topic again after the wedding. I am concerned about starting off our marriage with her feeling distressed."

"I'm sure it's natural," Charles offered. "She's young –."

"Not really," Oliver reminded him. "She was never really afforded the opportunity to be young."

Charles thought for a moment. "I suppose you are right. But getting married is an overwhelming thing. And she will be leaving her home. Her brother, her sister, their children. It's a big change."

"We won't be far from them, if it is that."

"Yes, but it's a change all the same," Charles countered.

"Hmm," Oliver finished the last of the brandy in his glass, his gaze back on the fire as he considered it. He didn't quite believe it was as simple as that.

"She is comfortable with you, though she may need time to adjust to each of your new roles. I imagine that will be simple enough for you two," Charles continued thoughtfully. "Is there anything you can do, though, to make her more contented in her new home? Even if that's not what's troubling her, or even the full of it, I am sure it would matter greatly to her and perhaps help."

A thought struck Oliver before Charles even finished speaking.

"Of course," he said, sitting up in his seat. "That's brilliant. I cannot believe it hadn't occurred to me before," he mumbled the last to himself.

Charles only smiled lightly at his younger brother, shrugging as he took another sip.

"What about you?" Oliver shifted his attention to Charles, while his mind wanted to run rampant with the plan it formulated for his new wife.

"Must you keep asking me?" Charles's smile vanished instantly as he looked away.

"It would do you wonders to follow your own sage advice, you know," Oliver stated the obvious. "Talk to your wife. Consider the overwhelming feelings she may be experiencing. The prospect of the upcoming change. Don't forget, she does not possess the benefit Genevieve and I do in that you two hardly know each other in any real way. And perhaps do something for her for once."

Charles only stared pensively into the fire, but Oliver knew his mind was working in the way he spun the glass between his fingers.

"Did you tell her she was beautiful the other night?" Oliver asked, trying to bring his brother out of his own head.

"I did," he said.

"And?"

"And she thanked me," Charles replied, making Oliver sigh. "She did look surprised," he admitted. "I don't think I have ever told her she was beautiful before."

"You don't *think*?" Oliver raised a brow.

"Very well, I *haven't* told her she was beautiful before," he ground out.

"You danced more than once. That's also progress. Why don't you try calling on her?"

"Damn it, Oliver," Charles snapped. He drained his glass before continuing, "It's different between us."

Oliver shook his head, completely frustrated at his brother's obstinance. He stood, placing his glass on the table beside the book he had not read. "It's different because you choose to make it so, but Anna deserves a husband willing to stand up and *be there* for her."

Not bothering to insist further, Oliver left to see to his own wife's needs as her husband should.

# CHAPTER 37

## GENEVIEVE

This was it. Her wedding day. Genevieve had spent all morning getting ready with the help of her maid and Amelia, and now she sat alone at her dressing table with nothing left to do but leave her bedroom.

It really hit her now. Oliver, her friend, that boy who gave a strange, quiet, scared little girl flowers and taught her how to skip rocks, how to leave the sheltered protection of her own mind, how to trust someone other than herself and rely on them…. That boy was about to become her husband. Three months ago, he had been gone. Gone for over seven years, and she had counted every moment of his absence never knowing if or when he would return. And now…. Now, he was back and forced to marry her.

He was still as kind, sweet, warm as ever. But would he come to resent her? Hate her for putting him in a position where he had to tie the rest of his life to hers because they were attracted to each other? Sure, attraction was putting it mildly, at least for her, and since he always matched her hunger in kind, she was rather confident he felt the depth of their pull, as well. But forever? Until death do they part? After seven years of boundless freedom, now shackled to the girl under the oak tree?

Genevieve trembled. She had to get a move on. If she sat here much longer letting these thoughts consume her, she'd do something *really* scandalous and try to set him free. And that was not an option.

Not only that, she knew and hated herself for the fact she didn't *want* to free him. That was her biggest shame. She wanted to marry him. She had only ever loved Oliver. With the limitlessness of a first love, the trust of a broken child, the might of a lifelong friend, the passion of a perfect lover. She would not let him go because he was all there was for her. All there had ever been for her. That's why she hated him so much when he left. Because without him, she was only half a person.

Genevieve stood and took one last look at herself in the full-length mirror. The dress had come together beautifully. Timeless and shapely, ending in the delicate designs crafted by her family's hands. She took a deep breath and blew it out slowly between her lips. Then she turned and walked out.

Gideon paced at the foot of the stairs. When he heard her coming, he looked up and stopped short. She kept her pace until she stood beside him and met his gaze. If she didn't know any better, she would say his green eyes looked particularly glassy.

"You look beautiful, Genevieve," he told her quietly.

"Thank you, brother," Genevieve gave him a nervous smile, which he understood perfectly.

"There's no need for nerves," he said, his voice firmer and demeanor back to its usual strong, composed presence. "Today will be one of your favorite memories."

"If you say so," she muttered, reaching for his arm, which he hadn't offered to her yet.

As she wrapped her hand gently around his forearm, he still did not turn to lead them out. Rather, he covered her hand with his own.

"Genevieve," he said solemnly. "Before we go, I need you to understand something."

Her face pulled in confusion and concern at the gravity she heard in his tone. She nodded, urging him to continue.

"This is your home. No matter what happens, no matter what the reason, you can always, *always* come home. You needn't ask. You needn't share anything you do not wish to. Wherever I am, there is always a place beside me that is yours and yours alone. I don't care about a scandal." He shook his head in response to the incredulous look he correctly read on her face. "Truly, I don't. If you did not love the man and he did not love you, I would never have insisted on this wedding. I would have found a different solution – I am the Duke of Birmingham after all," he smirked arrogantly before continuing once again in the same sober manner. "I would have kept you from harm, Genevieve. I will always keep you safe."

Genevieve could not believe what he was saying. They forced Oliver for nothing?

"If you ever need or want to come home, for a day, a week, a year, forever, you come home. Do you understand me?" His voice was firm.

Genevieve felt a lump form in the back of her throat, making it impossible for her to respond right away, but his expression made clear they would not be moving a single step until he had his answer.

She cleared her throat. "I understand," she said quietly.

Gideon gave a single nod, satisfied, and kissed her forehead.

"Let's not keep everyone waiting any longer, then," he said, finally walking them to the door. "We're already rather fashionably late."

"I am the bride," Genevieve's throat was still thick from the emotions running through her at his words. "I can be as late as I please."

"I don't think that is *entirely* accurate, but I understand your sentiment."

They made their way into the carriage, and within minutes, they were at the church. Genevieve's heart pounded like it was trying to break free of her chest and make a run for it. She felt a fresh wave of fright when the carriage finally came to a standstill, and she realized the only thing left to do was to actually marry Oliver. He was already here. Waiting for her inside this very building.

The footman opened the carriage door, but Gideon grabbed her hand instead of exiting. She yanked her attention from the church to her brother's face.

"You love him, don't you?" Gideon asked, his voice low and genuine.

"More than anything," she answered honestly.

He smiled warmly, pleased. "Then don't keep him waiting."

# CHAPTER 38

## OLIVER

Oliver was ready. He was so, *so* ready to marry Genevieve. His life had been bound to hers from the moment they met thirteen years ago. Now, the world would finally know it, too.

He sat in the front pew of the church, breathing in the scent of warm incense that did nothing to calm him. His leg bounced up and down. He couldn't stop it. The guests were lucky he wasn't running circles around the lot of them in an attempt to expel some of this nervous, excited energy coursing in his blood.

Then Oliver heard them. The doors were opening, the servants were readying, and the priest was stepping into place signaling for Oliver to join him. He looked to his brother seated beside him, who smiled, amused at whatever he saw on Oliver's face, but Oliver could not care less at whatever it was. She was here. Finally, *finally* here. He hadn't seen her in eleven full days, and now she was here to marry him.

Charles clapped him on the shoulder and stood up, and Oliver realized he still sat like an idiot. He stood, taking his place at the altar and facing the door currently separating him from Genevieve, the priest on his one side, his brother on the other.

The large double doors opened, and Anna stepped forward. Oliver was pleased. Of all the people she could have asked to stand with her, his wife had chosen Anna. Because she was her friend. Because they would soon be family. Because his smart, caring wife was determined to set up his brother and future sister-in-law, even using the opportunity their own wedding conveniently presented.

Oliver smiled at the pretty redhead as she walked down the aisle. She smiled back at him before her eyes moved to Charles. Oliver didn't look over to see what expression his brother wore, but whatever it was, it kept Anna's gaze fixed on him until she reached the altar and took up her place.

Then all other thoughts left Oliver's mind.

There she was. Beautiful and elegant, shining with soft brightness in the palest pink-white dress. She was blushing, he noted with happiness. He could count on one hand the number of times Genevieve had ever blushed. Her hair sat styled atop her head, jewels sparkling along her neck and ears. In her hand, she clutched a bouquet of foxgloves. The first flower he ever gave her. The flower that started this all.

She was the loveliest sight he'd ever beheld, and he could not look away. Even if his life depended on it, he could not look away. And her eyes, black and depthless, did not waver from him either.

As she and her brother approached him, he noticed more of the dress. How it hugged her shape, how her breasts pushed delicately against the neckline. He wanted to run his hands over the length of the silk before he ripped it off her with his teeth at the center of her breasts. But that dress was too beautiful. She was too perfect in it to ever do such a thing.

Finally reaching the altar, Oliver took the hand Gideon

offered him with a nod before his new brother backed away and took his place beside the duchess in the front pew.

"Good morning," Genevieve greeted him, and he was desperate, so unbelievably desperate to kiss her, hug her, simply hold her.

"My gem," he answered instead, unable to resist pulling her hand to his lips and kissing it before he turned to make his vow. To join his life with hers for everyone to see.

It was surreal, listening to the priest, feeling Genevieve's hands in his, her fathomless eyes on him. She didn't smile, just stared at him like he was the center of her world, and he understood. She was the center of his, too.

They repeated the words the priest directed, and Oliver placed his maternal grandparents' wedding ring on her finger. Then he was *finally* allowed to kiss her.

Oliver pulled her to him by their joined hands, lifting them up for her to wrap her arms around his shoulders before he let go to grip her waist. And then his lips were on her. He gave a low groan, just for her to hear, as he finally had her against him again. He missed her lips, her taste, her scent. He missed everything about her.

Drawing his lips from hers, he moved them to her ear and made one final vow, just for them. "I swear, not another day will go by when I am not with you, Genevieve. From now until we die, I will stay with you, be with you, each and every day. We will live and leave this life together."

Genevieve answered by wrapping her arms around his shoulders again and holding him to her with all the strength she had in her body. He did the same, keeping her close and feeling her heart beat against his chest, hoping she felt his, too.

And with that, they were married.

They had to break apart, as much as he hated letting her go. He kept a firm grip on her hand, though, one she matched. Making their way back down the aisle, they exited the church surrounded by their happy guests and entered the carriage that would take them back to Birmingham House for their wedding breakfast.

"So," Genevieve said as the carriage began to move. "We're married."

"We are," Oliver couldn't stop smiling. He lifted the hand still held tightly in his to place another kiss upon it. Then he met those beautiful dark eyes and growled, "To hell with it," before cupping her head gently and pulling her to him. He kissed her again, this time with more of the passion they shared.

As the kiss started to take on a life of its own, she pushed him away. "We still have guests to meet," she reminded him, slightly breathless.

He sighed and fell back against the cushioned seat, but he still couldn't hide away the smile refusing to leave his face. "Very well, wife," he replied, practically beaming at her.

Genevieve laughed. "Is that what you'll call me instead from now on?" she asked.

"Instead?" he repeated in question, and then understood. "Oh, no, you will always be my gem. Only now, you are little Gen. My gem. My wife."

She watched him, something between amusement and curiosity in her gaze, before she chuckled. "I suppose I am, husband."

And damn it, but he had to kiss her.

# CHAPTER 39

## GENEVIEVE

The morning went by in a blur, overwhelming Genevieve with everything. People greeting her and offering well wishes. The emotions from what Gideon had divulged. The excitement of the ceremony, and the peace of Oliver's whispered vows. Her guilt, her joy. She'd never felt so contrary and complex before in her life. Through it all, Oliver did not left her side. He was a constant presence, a hand always at her back or holding hers or tucking it into the crook of his elbow.

Before she knew it, it was all over, and she and Oliver were stuffed back into their carriage and off to honeymoon in her new country home, Sinclair Manor.

"What a morning," the words sighed out of her as the carriage began to jostle through the streets.

"A good one, I hope," Oliver took her hand and kissed the back of it gently. He'd been doing that all day. His deep ocean blue eyes were on hers as she watched him, trying to determine if it was his inherent kindness speaking or if he could perhaps be truly happy about their wedding.

"A very good one," she replied honestly, and his answering smile made her heart flutter in her chest.

"The best one," he agreed, putting his arm around her shoulders and pulling her against his chest.

Genevieve relaxed as she breathed in his cedar scent, letting it surround and comfort her as she rested her head on his shoulder, feeling the silk fabric of his coat against her skin. His other hand still held hers in his lap. She was exhausted. All the planning and emotions of the past few weeks, of the day, left her worn out and wrung. She was content here, in Oliver's arms, and very quickly her eyes drifted shut.

"Wife." Genevieve woke to Oliver planting kisses all over her face.

"What on earth," she sat up, disoriented. "What's going on? Where are we?"

"At the inn where we will be spending the night," he told her. She looked over at him to find his eyes bright with amusement. "You snore, you know."

"I most certainly do not," she replied indignantly. "And a gentleman would not mention it if I did."

He leaned forward, invading her space, his lips a hairsbreadth from hers. She could taste the air he breathed, and that proximity alone made her want to moan and launch herself at him.

"I am no gentleman," he purred. "I am your husband."

The words slammed into her with her need, and she grabbed his coat and pulled him to her, crashing her lips against his. He finally returned her kiss the way she wanted for the first time that day. For the first time since the garden. He was ruthless, and so was she. Her body immediately responded, growing warm and tight, heating pooling between her thighs.

But instead of continuing, Oliver clasped her wrist, gently tugging her hand away as he moved back with a few light kisses before they parted fully.

"We are not finishing this in a carriage the first time, Gen," he said to her immense dismay. Of course, he was right, but also, she was desperate to have him. She pursed her lips, and he laughed, giving her another quick kiss. "Let's get settled and have some dinner."

They did exactly that and took their dinner in their room at the inn. Genevieve was filled with a jittery sort of excitement when she entered the warm space, the fire already blazing, and saw the large bed they would be sharing tonight. She loved that he hadn't even considered separate rooms or beds, and she was both nervous and eager for tonight. For what they had been leading up to for weeks. For what they would be doing in that very bed.

She found it difficult to eat, her buzzing energy distracting her from any hunger she might have been feeling. She *was* able to drink, and she sipped at her wine, embracing the warmth it spread through her. Genevieve made sure she still kept her head about her, though. She didn't want to miss a single second of what was to come.

"Will you tell me now?" Oliver brought her back to the present as he took another bite of his dinner. He sat across from her at the table in their room, eyes watching her as he chewed.

She sighed. Genevieve didn't pretend not to understand him. She knew exactly what he asked. In fact, she was surprised he had waited this long without bringing up their conversation at the park almost two weeks ago. She probably had her mother-in-law to thank for that since she kept them separated these past days leading up to the ceremony. Genevieve was grateful for it.

For one, her mother-in-law had been right. Seeing him at the church today to say their wedding vows after so many days apart made the moment all the sweeter.

For another, she didn't have to have *this* conversation in all that time. The one where she admitted her guilt and sought his forgiveness for shackling his life to her own. He would comfort her, because that's what he did, and it would make her feel all the worse.

She should tell him. She *had* to tell him. They were married now. And forced or not, guilty or not, they needed to do what was best for their marriage. Besides, if she couldn't tell Oliver, then who *could* she tell?

Genevieve took another, slightly more generous, sip of her wine and placed it back on the table. She looked up and met his deep blue gaze. He tried to be nonchalant, but his worry was clear as he continued to watch her, waiting. She didn't look away as she spoke.

"I am sorry," she said, her voice strong and sincere. "I am sorry for what happened in that garden. For initiating it and thinking we would not be found. I am deeply, deeply sorry for trapping you into marriage. I was not trying to," she assured him, needing him to understand that immensely vital fact. "I was overcome by my desire for you, and I simply did not think. About someone finding us. About what that would mean. About what you would then have to do. I have been plagued with guilt since. Guilt that I caused this. That I forced your hand. That…." Her voice finally wavered, and she dropped her eyes to her plate. But she made herself say the words. "That I am *happy* about it. About being wed to you."

Her words left her abruptly. Because that was it. That was the real crux of what weighed upon her. It wasn't just that she was the reason they were caught. Or that she had put Oliver in a position where he had to marry her. The guilt of that would have been more than sufficient. But the thing that overwhelmed her constantly and sat on her chest like an immovable weight was that she was happy. She was excited to marry to him. She *wanted* to marry him. The guilt of that absolutely crushed her.

"And the absolute worst of it is that Gideon told me today you needn't have married me at all. He would have found another way to keep me untouched by scandal," she told him the final piece of it, finally expelling all of her confession. She reached once again for her wine, hoping it would wash away the burning she felt at the back of her throat and in her eyes.

Genevieve still couldn't look at him. Couldn't bear to see his shock from Gideon's proclamation, the regret, or worse, the sympathy as he lied to her and told her it was alright. So, she took a sip, staring at the fire, then curled her glass against her chest for the inevitable moment when she would need another.

What she had not been expecting as she waited, however, were the words he practically spat at her from across the table.

*"You are a fucking idiot."*

# CHAPTER 40

## OLIVER

*O*liver could strangle her. Not that he would ever do anything to harm her, physically or otherwise, but it was the sentiment. He couldn't ever remember being angrier with her.

"Excuse me?" Genevieve finally met his eyes again, and he saw the fire blazing there.

"You heard me," he retorted, adding, "And you can save the indignation for when you actually have a leg to stand on."

"What are you talking about?" Her brows narrowed, but the stubborn streak in her eyes had yet to dissipate. She put her glass back on the table, reminding Oliver that he, too, had wine.

He yanked up his own cup and took a large drink.

This woman. *This woman.*

He forced himself to take a deep breath and expel it before he focused back on her and tried to not be as enraged as he was. It barely worked.

"That's probably the dumbest thing you've ever said, Genevieve," he attempted to speak calmly but had a feeling it just sounded like he ground his words out through clenched teeth. Because he did. "Not just to me, but to anyone."

"You're being an ass," she told him.

"Rightfully," he almost yelled. "First of all, if I did not want to marry you, I never would have kissed you to begin with. Not just in that garden, but by the lake. Or during the Gardiner's Ball. I wouldn't have put my hands all over you like I could never get enough. I would never have shoved my face between your legs hellbent on hearing you scream my name."

He noticed the fire in her eyes straddle that perpetually fine line of anger and lust between them. His own fury shifted its energy slightly, too.

"I *want* you to be happy marrying me. I have been in an unending state of bliss for the past two and a half weeks at the prospect of having you as my wife. Of being your husband. I'll be damned if I'm in that alone. You did not trap me into anything. I've wanted you from the moment I returned and saw the little girl that is and has always been my best friend turned into this stunning, seductive, beautiful spitfire of a woman that I knew was hidden inside. Even when I wanted to toss you into the lake or damn near smother you, I wanted you desperately. I would have courted and married you anyway if you had not been the sister of a duke that I was sure deserved to marry someone with a title."

"What?" Her face pulled into disgust.

"It's beside the point," he brushed her question aside. "Charles and Gideon made me see how foolish I had been. I must say, I did not expect you to put my foolishness to shame, though. I told you a long time ago, any man would be lucky to marry you. Did you think I lied? *No man* need be forced to marry you, *least* of all me. How can you not see that you are my soulmate?" His anger simmered down in favor of disbelief. "That I am so madly, deeply, inconceivably in love with you. That I am and will forever be only yours."

A pause followed, and Genevieve only stared at him, eyes skeptical, lips parted as if shocked by his words and trying to determine their sincerity. Oliver shook his head and took another sip of his wine, placing the glass down gently before meeting her eyes again.

"As I said," he finished. "You are an idiot."

The words cracked through whatever shock encased her, and she launched herself at him. He grabbed her by the waist and pulled her down onto his lap as he held her close. Her fingers tangled aggressively into his hair in that way that made him immediately rock hard for her. Her lips were on his, and she took no prisoners. She was rough and unleashed, and he deepened the kiss, matching her fervor. She pulled hard at his roots, while his fingers bruised her hips, her waist, her back, as he made his way up her dress.

Oliver pulled at her ties just as she tore at his waistcoat, shoving it off. Then she yanked at his cravat, while he pulled her dress down off her shoulders. He broke their kiss to start unlacing her stays, and she took the opportunity to unbutton and remove his shirt. He loved the way she didn't shy away from her desire. That she was not ashamed of it. That she wanted, *needed* him as desperately as he did her, and she did everything in her power to satiate that need. She was fucking glorious.

Oliver pushed her gently off him, encouraging her to stand, so he could finish undressing her. Genevieve took the hint, letting her clothes fall to the floor, standing there in only her chemise. She pulled it off her shoulders before tugging the pins from her hair just as he stood and began removing his breeches and the last of his clothing.

Once they were both naked, their clothes pooled at their feet, they both simply stood there for a few moments, eyes devouring each other in the light from the fire. She was incredible. Porcelain skin that he wanted to trace and memorize with his fingertips. Delicate breasts he was desperate to mark with his teeth. Long black hair he wanted wrapped around his fist to pull hard as he rode her from behind.

And that was the thought.

Within a heartbeat, he was on her. His grip punishing, making her cry out in a moan, while she tried to rip his skin off him in return. His mouth wasted no time, seizing the opportunity of her moan to kiss and lick down her neck. He gently bit the sensitive skin where her pulse beat a rapid rhythm before lifting her up. Genevieve's legs wrapped instinctively around his waist and brought his cock right to the warm, inviting apex of her thighs as he walked them over to the bed and laid her down. He covered her body with his own. It would be so easy. One little shift of his hips, and he'd be buried right where he wanted to be. Right in that tempting heat.

But no. Not yet.

First, he would see to his wife.

# CHAPTER 41

## GENEVIEVE

Genevieve was *on fire*. Her blood pounded through her tightened skin. Her breasts felt full and heavy, and her core ached. She could not get close enough to him. To her husband. To Oliver. He was everywhere, his magnificent body hovering over her, all hard planes and honed muscles. He surrounded her, his taste on her tongue, his scent in her air, his mouth on her skin. She needed more. She wanted to give him more. She wanted to give him what he had given her before.

He moved down her body, reaching her breasts, one hand cupping her and pinching her nipple, while his mouth and tongue, and oh, his *teeth*, bit at the other. He wasn't gentle, and it was perfect. She cried out again, arching further into him, as he purred against her skin, "That's it, little Gen. Let me hear you."

"Not yet," she panted. Shoving him back, she moved until he lay on the bed with her straddling him. "It's my turn to hear you, *husband*."

Leaning forward, Genevieve kissed the edge of his jaw, where his beard met his neck, and moved down. She delighted in his groan and rapid heartbeat under her palm as he understood her intent. "You'll have to tell me what you like," she whispered against the muscles of his tanned and taut chest. The dusting of hair made her toes curl. He was just so masculine. It satisfied an urge within her she hadn't even noticed possessing.

She wanted to bite the firmness of him, and so she did. Oliver let go of the sheets and grabbed her backside instead, hard enough for her to know she'd have a bruise in the shape of his handprint tomorrow. The thought made the fire raging within her burn even brighter.

His muscles were chiseled and carved from his years of adventures. He was so beautiful. Every inch of him. Including his cock, which she finally reached and admired. With one hand, she stroked him the way she knew he liked, her grip firm and moving slowly up and down his hot, velvety skin. He was hard, so hard under her fingers, so deliciously thick and long. She licked her lips in anticipation.

"*Fuck*, the way you're looking at me," he groaned. She hadn't realized he'd been watching her. "It's like you're dying to have me in your mouth."

"I am," she murmured and covered the tip with her lips. She swirled her tongue over him, opening her mouth further to take him deeper. Keeping her hand fisted around the base of his length, she began matching the movement of her mouth with it, trying to find her rhythm. She listened to his groans and pants as signals of what to continue, what to repeat.

"That's it," he panted breathlessly. "Squeeze the tip, gem." She eagerly did his bidding as her hand stroked him in tandem with her mouth, and he rewarded her with his deep, guttural groan.

Oliver stopped using words, and she took that to mean he was losing himself to the pleasure she gave him. When she started moving faster, one of his hands grabbed the back of her hair and gripped it hard, directing her and setting an unforgiving pace. Genevieve let him, only too excited to give him the euphoria he had given her when it was his head between her thighs.

As if the memory had left her mind and gone straight into his, Oliver removed his hand, reaching instead for her legs. She kept her mouth on him, trying to maintain her rhythm and understand what he was doing.

A moment later, she knew, as he yanked her legs up, turning them onto their sides on the bed, and latched onto her clit.

She moaned in shock and pleasure at the intensity with which Oliver devoured her, his cock still in her mouth. Her legs wrapped around his head as she pushed into his face, the powerful strokes of his tongue on her sensitive bud driving her wild. Genevieve lost complete control and channeled her pleasure on his cock, her mouth moving faster, her cries muffled by its fullness. His answering groans vibrated against her, pushing her further and further.

Her teeth scraped him gently as she squeezed his tip with each hard, tight, wet stroke. Oliver bit her in turn just as he plunged two fingers inside her. He curved them on the way out, and she knew he was driving her with a vengeance to her orgasm. She couldn't keep her rhythm anymore, trembling in his arms as she released him from her mouth, panting. She still kept her hand on him, though, and when he bit down again, she came with a cry of his name.

"You are so sweet," he purred, removing his fingers and licking along her seam. He unwound her legs from around his head and sat up on his knees. "And so wet for me. Was that what sucking me did to you?"

"Yes," she answered as he licked his fingers clean. The sensual sight made her shiver and dart her own tongue across her lips as she watched. She sat up and pushed him down onto his back again. His hands landed possessively on her thighs, while she splayed one of hers onto his chest with equal possession. She reached between them with the other for his mouthwatering length. "You're just as sweet. I cannot help it," she murmured seductively, causing his fingers to flex against her skin. One hand moved up to cup her breast, teasing her nipple. "You'll have to help me," she said as she moved to position him, but the action ran the tip of him along the length of her folds. It created such delicious, unexpected pleasure, her eyes shut involuntarily and she moaned before running his cock along her seam again.

"Fuck, you're exquisite," he growled, and her eyes opened to meet his hooded ones. Those blue eyes had never looked so dark before, and she believed him. Genevieve felt like the most beautiful, most desirable, most goddamn exquisite thing that had ever existed. "I love the way you want me." He moved both of his hands to brush the hair back from her face and hold it at her nape. "Like you can't control yourself." He sat up, reaching for her lips with his own, but instead of kissing her, he took her bottom one between his teeth before rasping, "Like I want you."

She took those words as permission and lowered herself onto him as much as she could. Oliver dropped his hands to her hips, adjusting her angle in a way that allowed her to take him in more. When his length pushed up against the thin barrier within her, he wrapped his arms tightly around her back, bringing her chest flush with his, one hand shoved into her hair to cradle her head as he kissed her deeply. He thrust his hips up just as he pulled her down, ripping gently through her virginity and causing her to gasp into his mouth.

The pain subsided quickly, and Genevieve was left only with the delicious fullness of him within her. *This.* This is what she had been aching for, for weeks now. Oliver inside her, filling her, stroking her, completing her. With each shift of her hips and matching thrust of his own, she felt herself growing manic. Her fingers clawed at his shoulders as uncontrollable moans erupted from her with each stroke, getting louder and louder. She shoved him back down with her palms flat on his shoulders as she turned into pure instinct. With him once again flat beneath her, she dug her fingers into the delectable muscles of his chest and rode his cock with an animalistic ferocity she hadn't known existed within her.

She was starting to lose her pace again, her muscles growing so taut that she was shaking, but she continued to move her hips as she desperately climbed the wave within her. Oliver's thrusts were deep and sure, and when he lifted one of his hands from her hips and brought it down with a sharp slap against her ass, she came harder than she ever had before, head thrown back as a scream tore through her.

Genevieve barely made it down to earth when Oliver had their positions flipped, his body covering hers. He pounded into her, driven by his own madness, before he groaned deep in his chest, his cock twitching inside her and filling her.

They were both out of breath. Both panting and sweaty. She traced her fingers along his spine, his head tucked into the crook of her neck.

"So, you love me?" she asked cheekily, but really just wanting to hear it again.

He lifted his head from her shoulder to meet her eyes and then broke out into laughter. She did, too, her heart, body, and soul beyond full.

"More than life, itself, Gen," he chuckled before kissing her with such tenderness, she was sure she would burst.

# CHAPTER 42

## OLIVER

It had been the best day of his life, and after last night, Oliver was sure nothing could make him happier. Then he woke up to Genevieve sleeping peacefully beside him, and he had to admit he'd been wrong. He could not believe this was now his life. They were married. She was an enthusiastic, passionate, insatiable lover, who practically ravaged him three times the night before, before finally collapsing from exhaustion. He would spend every day of the rest of his life waking up to her delicate face, surrounded by a mess of black silk hair, and peaceful breaths.

Oliver leaned forward and kissed her lips very, very gently.

"Will you always do that?" she muttered, irritated.

He chuckled. Of course, his gem was a grouch in the mornings.

"Probably," he answered honestly.

She cracked her eyes open, her black marbles finding him before she harrumphed and turned over. He took the advantage and began pressing kisses onto her back and along her shoulders.

"Time to wake up, my wife, my gem," he said between kisses.

"That's not how it goes," she mumbled into her pillow.

"I am still testing out the order I like best," he explained. "Come on, let's get ready and continue on our journey to the Manor." He smacked her bottom through the sheet, making her yelp, and stood up.

That caught his vixen of a wife's attention as she lifted her head, peering over her shoulder to watch his naked body move about the room.

Catching her eye, he smirked. "I am glad you admire my body so much, and I hope you intend to make frequent use of it, so I need not feel guilty for doing the same to you."

"Come back to bed, and I will make use of it right now," she purred in a sultry, sleep-rasped voice that made his cock twitch.

"I do that, and we won't make it back to the Manor at all before we're expected back in London," he replied truthfully.

Heaving a great put upon sigh, Genevieve finally got out of bed. Before long, they were dressed and on their way to Birmingham, where they would spend the next month in blissful solitude.

Three days later, they reached Sinclair Manor in the late afternoon, having spent the majority of their trip wrapped up in each other and making love both at night and during the day in the cramped carriage. They looked a little worse for wear by the time they stepped out of it in Birmingham, but the staff would either assume it was the long journey or they'd forgive them their newlywed joy.

The servants all waited for them in a line in front of the Manor and smiled happily at the new young mistress of the house that had already been a frequent visitor there these past years. Oliver did not let her dawdle or speak to anyone yet, however, too excited for what came next. He took her hand and led her hurriedly up the steps and into her new home.

Moving quickly through the lovely, white walled entry hall without stopping, he glanced around at the perfectly kept interior with its bright paintings and flowers. He spoke his thoughts out loud as they walked. "We can get our own house. We don't need to stay here."

He didn't care where they lived, but he was partial to staying close to his family and hers, as he knew she was, too. But they'd likely want a place of their own, at least eventually.

"Perhaps one day," she replied, mirroring his line of thinking. "Maybe once Charles and Anna are married. So, we can give them some space," she offered, following him without question as he led her to the drawing room.

"I think that's a wonderful plan," he smiled sidelong at her as he opened the finely crafted white door, guiding her to enter first. "We'll have to be sure to take this with us, though, of course."

Genevieve stopped dead in the doorway, preventing him from entering further, which suited him just fine. He wrapped his arms around her waist, hugging her back to his front, as he lowered his head to the crook of her neck, resting his chin on her shoulder. He whispered softly, "Welcome to our first home together, Mrs. Sinclair."

"Oliver," she breathed in disbelief, still unmoving.

"Go, have a look," he instructed, placing a kiss where her neck and shoulder met, then releasing her.

Genevieve took small, hesitant steps until she finally reached the new grand piano sitting in the room. Oliver followed close behind, letting her set the pace. She reached one hand out and caressed the shining wood reverently. Walking slowly around it, she lifted the lid and stroked the keys with the same deference.

"You bought me my own grand piano?" Her voice was so quiet, her eyes not meeting his, and for a moment, he worried he might have somehow made a mistake.

"Yes," he answered cautiously.

"No one has ever done anything like this for me," she whispered, almost to herself with her head still tilted down, looking at the keys beneath her fingertips.

"I will do anything for you," he vowed, and he meant each word as he tried to gauge her reaction.

Finally, she looked up, and he saw the tears sliding down her cheeks.

"I love you, Oliver," she said, black eyes staring deeply into his, not letting him go.

He stepped forward, a hand cupping her cheek while the other pulled her to him by the waist. He kissed her with all the love they'd built over the last thirteen years. Genevieve wrapped her arms around him and kissed him back with a mixture of love, laughter, and tears.

Pulling back, he lifted his other hand to her face, as well, and wiped her tears as she continued to laugh and cry.

"I love you, Gen," he murmured, letting her see and hear the truth on his face, in his words. "Now, play something for me, and then you and I are going to the lake."

"The lake? This late?" she asked, her beautiful face still split into its breathtaking smile, eyes glistening with joyful tears.

"Yes." He nodded seriously before leaning down to brush his lips against hers and whisper in a low voice, "It's been far too many years since you and I have been able to enjoy a swim together, my gem."

# CHAPTER 43

## GENEVIEVE

"*O*liver, are you sure about this?" Genevieve asked, holding her husband's hand as he led them towards the familiar oak tree nearby. She'd never approached their place from this angle; it was slightly surreal, and she loved it. "It will be dark soon."

"That's why we packed candles," he smirked at her over his shoulder. The sight made her heart beat a little erratically. Goodness, that smirk. Would she ever become immune to it?

They crossed the grass towards the spot where they first met. While she had played a new piece for him, reflecting the happiness she felt from their love, he had asked the staff to pack up their dinner so they could eat it as a picnic under their oak tree. Now, in the hand not holding Genevieve's, Oliver carried a basket full of food, wine, and apparently candles, as well as two sheets tossed over his forearm.

She could not deny the delight she felt at his spontaneity and his desire to have her all to himself. He really was happy being married to her. It hadn't seemed possible before their wedding that he could be as happy as she was given the circumstances that led to their nuptials. With the past few days and finally talking to him, she could see things clearly without the blinders of her own guilt and distrust of life. Oliver was completely right on their wedding night. She had been an idiot.

Genevieve wished she'd talked to him about everything sooner. It had made perfect sense at the time to hold back, but again, those had been her old, poisonous habits that she had been forced to rely on for far too long. But this was Oliver. She needed to remember once again that when it came to this man, there was never a reason to hold back. He was a part of her. Her other half.

She never imagined she could be this happy.

They came up to the oak tree, and Oliver paused only long enough to deposit the basket before continuing to pull her towards the lake. Stopping beside it, he turned to face her, grinning like an absolute fool. Genevieve laughed at the sight.

He let go of her hand and dropped the sheets in the grass before shrugging off his coat.

"Strip," he said as he began unbuttoning his waistcoat and discarding it with everything else on the ground.

Genevieve arched a silent brow, her lips pulling up into a grin of her own.

"Impatient, husband?" she asked, unpinning her hair before shifting the length of it over one shoulder and turning around for him to help with the ties at her back. He already had his shirt halfway unbuttoned, pulling it out of his breeches, when he stopped and attended to her dress in quick order. When he finished and she began turning back around, he yanked her to him in a searing kiss.

"You have no idea, wife," he practically growled against her lips. He rubbed his nose against hers before pulling back and finishing the buttons on his shirt. "Ever since I saw you swimming here all those weeks ago, I have wanted you naked in this water."

"You might've said," she teased, taking off her dress and working on removing the rest of her clothing.

Oliver only scoffed in reply, clearly in far too much of hurry to even bother bickering with her. Genevieve laughed again.

A moment later, they were completely undressed, and Oliver was on her. He wrapped his arms tightly around her, hugging her close as he kissed her savagely. Genevieve's amusement remained, but that perpetual fire that burned inside her for her husband blazed beside it. Clearly, this had been something he fantasized about many times. The thought made her smile, even as her body became soft and ready for him.

She reached up and pulled his face away from hers with a hand in his hair, the other pushing him back at his shoulder. Those blue eyes found hers, and their color was even darker with the evident hunger shining through them. Oliver looked at her like a man starved, even though they'd made love multiple times daily for the past several days.

She smirked at him and nipped playfully at his bottom lip before she unlocked his arms from around her, turned, and dove into the lake. She broke back through the surface to find Oliver already in the water beside her.

Genevieve wasn't sure who reached for whom, but a moment later, she had her arms around his neck, the fingers of one hand splaying into his hair. His hands were around her back again in that punishing grip of his. She kissed him roughly, like she would devour him. She didn't know if this feeling would ever stop, this heady desire to consume every bit of him, to burn together in the heat of their passion.

Instinctively, she lifted a leg and wrapped it around his hip, pulling his hard cock to her center, where her body still craved him most, completely unsated from the many hours of attention it had already received.

Oliver pulled back and looked down at her body beneath the water. He lifted a hand and traced her nipple with his index finger. She shivered in his arms, tugging his hair at the sensitive pleasure of it.

"I loved that you still swam," he murmured, still looking at where his finger caressed her. Then he cupped her breast and pinched her nipple roughly, making her moan and throw her head back. Oliver's eyes lifted to her face and watched her like he was memorizing each of her reactions. "When I came upon you that day. I loved that you still swam." His hand abandoned her breast and reached up to cup her chin, his thumb rubbing back and forth against her skin.

She panted slightly as she lowered her hand from his hair and let it rest gently on his shoulder. Her voice was a rasp when she spoke, "How could I not? My husband taught me." Then she shifted her hand to the nape of his neck and squeezed while she captured his lips in an aggressive and demanding kiss.

The sun had almost set, and the two of them were still wrapped around each other, not bothering to swim at all. Instead, they attacked one another with their hands, mouths, teeth, until she couldn't take anymore and whispered against his mouth, "I need you, Oliver." The words seemed to gratify something within him, because he bit her lip with a groan. He gently disentangled his limbs from hers and pulled her back to the edge of the lake.

Climbing out, he kept a firm hold on her hand as he bent and grabbed one of the sheets he'd brought. In the semi-darkness, he walked her over to the base of the oak tree, where a kind little boy once asked a broken little girl her name. And there, amongst its strong roots, a husband bent his wife over, a fist wrapped around her hair, their moans music in the air, as they lost themselves to passion and love and forever.

# CHAPTER 44

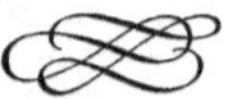

## OLIVER

"So, where did you go?" Genevieve asked. Her body was relaxed and loose as she looked at him from across the sheet where they now finished their meal. He was glad he thought to bring two of them, since the first was thoroughly soaked from when they'd taken each other still wet from their swim. It now lay crumpled and discarded next to the empty picnic basket beside them.

Genevieve sat in her chemise and wearing his coat, while he had redressed in only his shirt and breeches. He couldn't deny the masculine feeling of triumph within him at the sight of her. She held the coat closed with one hand, her glass of wine sparkling in the candlelight in her other. Oliver watched her from where he lay back, propped up on one elbow. Genevieve, his wife, took his breath away.

"Did I go somewhere?" he asked, trying to focus on her words instead of her beauty.

She rolled her eyes at him before replying in a mocking tone, "Were you only hiding in the Manor for seven years?"

"Oh," he laughed. "That."

"Yes, that," she said, trying and failing to hide her smile.

"All over," he told her. "France, Belgium, Germany, Denmark, Greece. I actually wrote it all down for you in my diary as I traveled, everything I wanted to tell you."

"You did?" Her face was so shocked, he couldn't help but chuckle.

"Of course, I did," he laughed again. "Did you think I wouldn't? I kept track of everything so I could share it with you when I came home."

"Why did you not tell me? Or better yet, give me your diary?"

"I had every intention to, but you were too busy fighting with me."

"I might not have fought with you quite so much if you had," she countered.

His mouth pulled up in a smirk as he had to concede, "That's very likely true."

"Well, until you give me your diary, which I expect the very moment we return home tonight, did you have a favorite place you visited?" she asked, taking a sip of her wine. He watched her throat swallow, his own mouth watering.

"Italy." He lifted his eyes back to hers to find them sparkling in the light from the candles, as if she knew exactly what he was thinking.

"Why Italy?"

"It was beautiful," he answered, unable to pull his eyes from the mischief in hers. He could not believe they were here. She was his wife. He would be looking at her stunning face for the rest of his days. First thing when he woke up. Last thing before he went to sleep.

"You're not paying attention," she remarked coolly, but obviously not upset.

"I can't help it," Oliver sat up, reaching over to cup her cheek, running his thumb along her soft skin. "I can't believe you're my wife, Gen."

She lifted her own hand from where she held his coat closed and clutched his wrist, turning her face to kiss his palm.

"I was always your wife, Oliver," she whispered, leaning her head into his hand. "I could never have been anyone else's."

And that was their most fundamental truth. The truth neither one of them had been capable of seeing until they were finally husband and wife, even if everyone else saw it. From the moment he found her in this very spot thirteen years ago, they were always headed here.

Oliver leaned forward and kissed her sweetly before withdrawing. He bent his knees and rested his elbows atop them as he faced her and answered properly.

"It was the architecture. The architecture, the art, the history, the culture in Venice, Rome, Florence. Especially Venice. It was surreal to see a city built on water. I learned more there than anywhere else and made most of my, *our*, fortune there. It's where I stayed the longest."

"It sounds wonderful," she smiled, her voice wistful.

"We'll go," he promised her. "And then you can see it for yourself."

Genevieve looked out towards the lake, which reflected the nearly full moon on its calm surface. She was quiet while she considered her thoughts, and Oliver just enjoyed watching her while he waited, the moving shadows on her face from the candlelight lighting her sharp, elegant features. He picked up his wine glass and took a drink without removing his eyes from his picturesque wife.

They were here, in the place that was theirs and theirs alone, in the moonlight. The experience was entirely singular, and Oliver was sure there had never been a happier or more contented moment in all his life.

"Not yet," she finally said, turning back to him.

"Oh?" he smirked at her.

"Anna and Charles's wedding is coming up," she clarified and then glanced down before meeting his eyes again.

His brows furrowed. "Is there something else?" he asked.

"Well," she cleared her throat and looked away from him. Oliver put down his glass as he waited for her to continue. "I would like a family with you first." Her voice did not waver, but when her eyes met his, he noted the nervousness buried in their dark depths.

"You mean children?" he confirmed.

"Yes," she replied. "I love George and Guinevere. And I want that. I want our children. Yours and mine. Whenever you're ready for them, too."

Yet, again, when he was absolutely certain he had achieved the peak of happiness, his fierce wife proved him wrong. He pounced on her, quickly taking the cup from her hand and tossing it, wine and all, to the side. He didn't care what he knocked over between them as he reached for her. All he knew was that he needed her in his arms immediately. He needed to convey the joy and love pounding through him. It needed a release, and she was it.

Oliver devoured her with his kiss as he pushed her back to the ground, covering her body with his. He couldn't stop kissing her, her jasmine scent assaulting his senses as her body writhed beneath him. He didn't pull back until they were both panting and out of breath. Lifting his head, he looked down into the fathomless eyes of the person he loved most in the entire world. He reached up to stroke her hair back from her face, before he finally answered, his voice rough and reverent.

"I am ready right fucking now, my gem."

# EPILOGUE

4 *months later*

"How much longer must we stay in London?" Oliver complained.

"Careful, darling," Genevieve teased as they walked up the steps of Birmingham House, her arm tucked in his elbow, and Charles and Prudence beside them. "You almost sound like you're whining."

"I *am* whining," he confirmed.

"Of all my children –."

"There's only two of us," Charles interrupted her.

"Of *both* my children," Prudence glared at him. "He's always been the one to most complain."

"I had more freedom to complain," Oliver nodded in agreement.

"How fortunate for you," Charles muttered as they stepped inside the Townhouse, greeting Lewis and then following him to the drawing room.

Entering the warm space with candles and firelight making the comfortable room glow, they were greeted by the other guests of tonight's intimate dinner. Genevieve let go of Oliver's arm to kiss Amelia where she stood up from the couch, while Oliver followed closely behind to greet Gideon. Prudence moved first, with a more hesitant Charles beside her, to greet Lord and Lady Dunhill and Anna.

Since they had returned to London, Oliver and Genevieve had been scheming with Amelia, Gideon, Lydia, Thomas, and Emily to find more opportunities for the stubborn couple to connect. It was slow going, to say the least, but they were making progress. They even leveraged the help of Philip, Alexander, Jack, and Grace, who were fast becoming a part of their group since the garden party. The ladies had also been trying to force enthusiasm into Anna, with the not-so-subtle help of Oliver's mother, in the wedding planning.

Tonight, however, they were having a small dinner with the closest relatives only, orchestrated by Amelia, which was why they were at Birmingham House. Genevieve's sister-in-law insisted, as did Prudence, that neutral territory and limited numbers might help the headstrong couple a bit more.

Now, they were all seated, having placed themselves strategically to leave space for Anna and Charles next to each other.

Genevieve, however, wasn't going to miss her chance before dinner. "Sister," she murmured to Amelia, squeezing her hand lightly. "Might I go to the nursery before dinner is called?"

Amelia's lips pulled up in a warm smile, and she leaned over to kiss Genevieve's cheek. "You need never ask," she said, turning back to Gideon and the group beside her. Gideon's emerald eyes smiled at Genevieve, too, as he tipped his head towards the door in a gesture to go on.

Oliver already waited since, when she turned to look at him, presumably to ask him to join her, he merely held out his hand. She smothered a laughing smile and took it. They heard Gideon promise the other guests the two of them would return shortly after seeing George and Guinevere.

George was beside himself when they entered the nursery,

and rather than run for his aunt, he bolted straight at Uncle Oliver's legs. Oliver scooped down before George could collide with his knees and picked him up, spinning him around.

"And how are you, little Lord?" he gave a small tickle to the toddler's belly, and George erupted into a fit of giggles while pushing Oliver's hand away.

"I am quite vexed with you, you know," Genevieve told Oliver, annoyed. "Good evening, Mrs. Potters," she greeted her old governess, who smiled, handing her a happy Guinevere. The nanny, then, left to give the couple some privacy with their niece and nephew. They had grown so much in the past six months since Oliver's return. "I used to be George's favorite," she finished, picking the thread of her statement back up as she sat in the armchair and bounced Guinevere on her knee. She placed a kiss atop her soft, velvety head of dark hair.

"You are a close second," Oliver informed her while he tossed the little boy into the air as he laughed and shrieked like it was the best day of his life.

"You'll be a *close second* with our own children," she told him, her tone insinuating it was something between a promise and a threat.

"We'll see." Oliver lowered George back to the ground, but the sweet little terror promptly grabbed his uncle's hand and pulled him towards his wooden rocking horse beside where Genevieve sat making faces at a giggling Guinevere. Oliver lowered to the ground beside the toy horse, keeping the enthusiastic George from flinging himself off it with a hand on his back.

"We'll *know* soon enough," she said and watched her husband's face as her message sank in.

Oliver's ocean eyes shot to hers in question, and her face broke into a grin. The next second, he was on his feet pulling her from the chair and wrapping his arms around her, careful not to crush Guinevere.

They were both laughing, and he cupped her cheek, staring into those magnificent black eyes that held the other half of his soul, and his deep blues the other half of hers. Her eyes were light and joyful and full of love. Mirroring his.

"Really?" he whispered, his tone reverent as his thumb brushed along the curve of her cheek.

"Really," she replied, her voice low, too.

Oliver leaned his forehead against Genevieve's, closing his eyes.

"I love you, my gem, my wife. Mother of my children."

She smiled, turning her head to kiss the palm of his hand.

"I love you, husband."

The End

# ACKNOWLEDGMENTS

This story is a particularly special one for me. It very much had a life of its own – I just held the pen as it wrote itself. So, I must start by expressing my deep and profound gratitude to those that helped make the story into a book. To Ayushi, Kaycee, and Maddi, thank you for your care and feedback on this book and its characters, who mean so much to me.

And as always, a very special thank you to Luisa for creating the absolute perfect cover.

Next, thank you to the folks that helped bring this book to readers. Thank you to Jane and the team at TorchLitInk. To Sierra and David, thank you for always inspiring and supporting me, and for the Bookery.

Finally, thank you to my readers for allowing me to share Genevieve and Oliver's story with you. I hope you enjoyed it as much as I did and that it stays with you in meaningful ways.

# ABOUT THE AUTHOR

K.P. March is a lover of literature, books, and the art of writing. She loves to lose herself in writing and reading books of dark romance, historical romance, romantasy, and fantasy, and she is an absolute sucker for happy endings. She studied Elizabethan Lit and holds a Ph.D. in Writing Studies. Originally from New Jersey, she now lives in the Cincinnati-area with her husband and three cats.

Follow K.P. March at:
www.authorkpmarch.com
www.instagram.com/authorkpmarch